TAINTED TRUTH

THE DEVILS OF NEW YORK

IVY KING

HEARTLEAF PUBLISHING LLC

Tainted Truth
The Devils of New York, Book 2
Published by Heartleaf Publishing LLC
Copyright © 2025 by Ivy King
All rights reserved.

Developmental Editing by Mara Montano - Mara's Editorial Services
Copy/Line Editing by Caitlin Lengerich
Cover Design by Echo Grace - Wildheart Graphics

 Created with Vellum

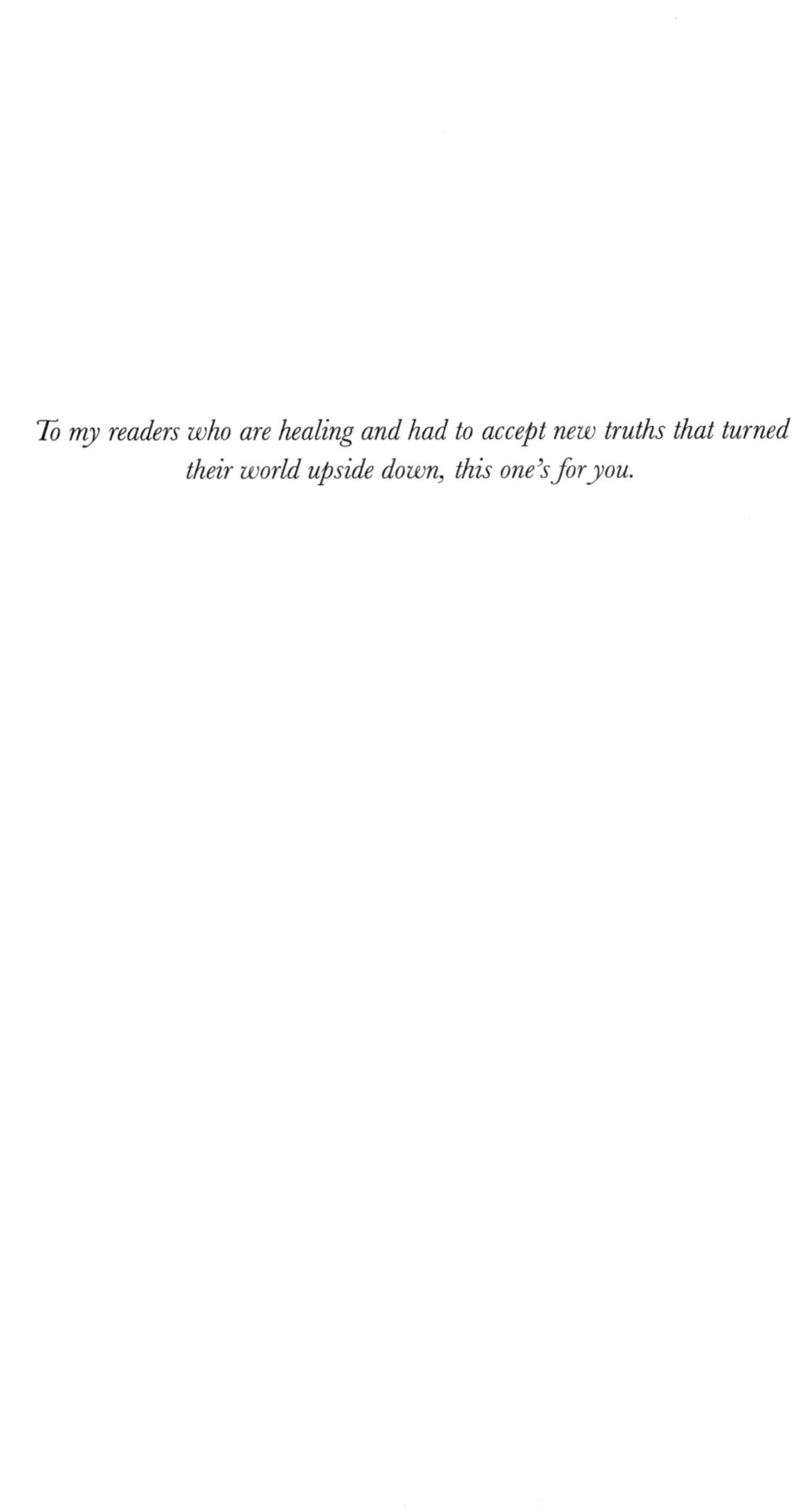

To my readers who are healing and had to accept new truths that turned their world upside down, this one's for you.

TABLE OF CONTENTS

TROPES & CONTENT WARNINGS

Tropes
Why choose, age gap, forced proximity, morally gray characters, suspense, feminine rage

Content Warnings
Handcuffs
Light CNC
Torture
Violence
Nightmares
Anxiety/Panic Attacks
Physical/Emotional Abuse (mentioned)
Rape & Attempted Rape
Stalking (not the romantic kind)
Manipulation/Gaslighting (not from the MMCs)
Details of a child's death
Details of child abuse

SPANISH TRANSLATIONS

Actúan como niños – You're acting like children

Buenas noches – good night

Cabrón – bastard

El hijo de puta no se aguanta – Son of a bitch still can't take a hit

Es ahí donde te equivocas, amigo – That's where you're wrong, friend

Está bien – He/She is good

Estamos locos – We're crazy

Hombre – man

¿Intentas matarme? – Are you trying to kill me?

Mara – gang

Mierda – shit

No dedos significa que no manejas – No fingers means no driving

No me gusta que lo necesitemos, pero lo entiendo – I don't like that we need him, but I get it

No quiero escucharlos – I don't want to hear it

Pendejo – asshole

Puedes pedir lo que quieras, y yo te lo daría – You can ask for anything, and I will give it to you.

¿Que pasa, hermano? – What's up, brother?
Si no estás de acuerdo, dilo – If you're not okay with that, you need to speak up now.
Te amo, mi corazón – I love you, my heart
Vamos, tórtolos – Come on, lovers
Y por qué fue eso – What was that for?
Ya está dormida – She's already sleeping

PLAYLIST

Toothbrush by DNCE
Talk (feat. Disclosure) by Khalid
Trumpets by Jason Derulo
Here With Me (feat. CHVRCHES) by Marshmello
Love Lies by Khalid & Normani
Be Kind by Marshmello & Halsey
Chains by Nick Jonas
Dirty Laundry by All Time Low
Nameless by Stevie Howie
lovely by Billie Eilish & Khalid
Control Freak by Doll Skin
Hands On Me (feat. Meghan Trainor) by Jason Derulo
Bad Dreams by Teddy Swims
White Roses by Glass Animals
Love The Hell Out Of You by Lewis Capaldi
Take Over (feat. Ruelle) by Hidden Citizens

PROLOGUE

SPENCER, SEVEN YEARS AGO

y palms sweat as I watch the analog clock on the wall tick with each passing second. I've never done this before—put myself out there. Abuela said she was proud of me when I called to tell her one of my sculptures had been chosen to be in a gallery. But now, here I am on opening night, and I'm a damn train wreck.

There are only a few minutes until the doors open, and Mom walked away to find the bathroom. Hopefully she'll be back soon because the butterflies in my stomach are out of control.

Mom and I bought a new dress for tonight, and while it's beautiful, it's too much for my taste. The deep red color compliments my skin, which is why Mom said we should buy it. The neckline is a deep V-cut, and the skirt hugs my ass and hips a little too much, but then falls away from my frame into an A-line skirt. Mom said it's just my body becoming more of a woman's body and less of a girl's body, but the leers from random men on my way here made my skin crawl.

I can't wait to get out of this annoying fabric when I go home tonight.

This gallery is known in Houston for discovering up-and-coming artists—many have gotten their big break here. All it takes is for the right rich dude to walk in, like an artist's work, pay an obscene amount of money for it, and tell all of their friends. Next thing you know you're getting commissions left and right.

I'm surrounded by fellow artists as we watch each other display our souls for the world to critique. There's everything from watercolor paintings to prints to ceramics.

When I arrived earlier, I noticed that we're all women. It's common for people to assume that art is a female-dominated industry, but the real artists know it's run by men. And because of that, I assumed I would see more classmates of mine, particularly of the male variety, but there are none.

The gallery went all out for this opening. Several waiters line the room with trays of hors d'oeuvres and flutes of champagne, and light instrumental music floats in the air. I'm sure all of their openings are just as fancy, but seeing it in person feels different.

I watch the gallery owner use his keys to open the door and welcome the large crowd gathered outside.

Where is Mom? I thought she'd be back by now.

God, I hope I don't fuck this up by being my usual awkward self.

As the room floods with people, I shrink back from the critical looks. I know I need to stand strong and be proud of what I created, but showcasing my work here is not the same as a presentation at school. When I'm there I'm being critiqued by my peers who have the same experience as me. Out here, in the real world, I'm talking to a prospective buyer. I need to be confident and sure of myself, but that level of surety is not a quality I have ever possessed.

Two middle-aged men in expensive black suits stand a few feet away from me and talk in hushed tones, but not so hushed I can't hear them. Their presence sends a chill down my spine.

"My last purchase didn't satisfy my needs like I thought she would." The man on the right chortles at his own statement.

The man on the left responds, "What a tragedy."

"I'm hoping the one I have my eye on tonight proves to be more useful."

As the man swipes an hors d'oeuvre from a passing waiter, he looks in my direction and gives me a once over. Then he pulls out his phone, presses a few buttons and slides it back into his pocket.

He takes a step in my direction and my chest grows tight, but another man makes it to my side first. He's older, and I swear he keeps trying to take a peep down the front of my dress. I try tugging on it in an attempt to hide my ample cleavage, but that doesn't work, and crossing my arms only serves to push my boobs up higher.

His hairline is receding, and his skin looks leathery, as if he's spent most of his time in the sun over the years. His suit is expensive and obviously tailored. He reminds me of the men Mom usually dates. The ones who take her to five-star restaurants, symphonies, and plays.

"What inspired you to create this . . ." He trails off as he waves to my sculpture of a minimalist, thin figure hunched over with its arms wrapped around its pathetic body. ". . . thing."

He steps closer and places a meaty hand on my lower back. A chill runs up my spine and I take a step forward, evading his touch.

I glance over my shoulder in search of Mom. She's usually good about running interference when a guy thinks I'm older than I am, but she's nowhere in sight.

My God, these creeps make me feel like I need to take a shower.

My words stumble out as I answer him. "He . . . Umm . . .

There was a homeless man I saw outside Bayou Music Center." Clearing my throat, I sidestep him when he attempts to make contact again.

My eyes roam the room in search of Mom one more time when I spot her in the corner talking to a gentleman resembling the one at my side.

Shit.

Mom deserves her happiness. She's a single mom and has provided for me my whole life. While my sperm donor's child support helps, I know she does what she must so I can have an easier life. Art school isn't cheap.

So, when I see her laugh and smile like that, I don't interrupt.

As I bring my gaze back to my piece, I make eye contact with one too many people.

If I can just find the damn bathroom, I can escape and hide until this geezer loses interest.

"Hugh, funny seeing you here. I didn't think you were in town." Another man in yet another suit stands opposite me. He holds a champagne glass, which looks dainty in his hand. His face is clean-shaven, and his light skin shines with a healthy glow. His nails are perfectly manicured, and his brows shaped. Thick mahogany hair styled with a natural look frames his face, but I see the tiniest glint of hair product. His sharp cheekbones and prominent jaw make him look harsh, but his eyes turn soft when they land on me.

I exhale a sigh of relief when Hugh's attention diverts from me, and he stops trying to get his hands on me.

"Anthony, dear friend, good to see you." Hugh's eye twitches slightly, but not slight enough that I don't catch it.

Hugh extends his hand, and they give each other a quick shake. When Hugh pulls away, he balls his fist at his side and his grasp on his glass turns white. I'm surprised it doesn't break.

Hugh turns to me and says, "Anthony here is always in attendance at these events. He . . . *acquires* more art than most." His hand makes its way to my arm and traces the length. My shoulders tense and I discreetly lean away.

Anthony slips a hand into his pocket and sips his drink with the other. He frowns at the space I placed between Hugh and I, and a flicker of hope lights inside me. I wish he would whisk me away from this creep.

Anthony is nice to look at and clearly more mature than the boys at school.

"Nonsense." His statement is directed towards Hugh. "You got that set of fine oil paintings from me just last month. I had my eye on those. They would have expanded my collection nicely."

"I can't say I'm sorry about that." A fake smile graces Hugh's mouth behind his own flute.

"Excuse us, we're being rude. I'm Anthony Cole." Anthony steps between Hugh and I, putting some much-needed space between us, and reaches his hand towards me.

Thankfully I've been to functions like this before with Mom, so I'm used to being dismissed and forgotten quickly.

I automatically grasp Anthony's hand. "Spencer Gray."

"Lovely to meet you, Ms. Gray." He unexpectedly guides my hand towards his lips, pulling me closer to him, and places a gentle kiss on my skin.

"Likewise," I return in a shaky voice.

Well this has never happened at a party before.

As he slowly lowers my hand, his eyes travel up and down my body. Chills erupt all over, and I'm not sure if it's a good or bad sign.

Anthony releases my hand and turns his attention to Hugh who is typing away on his phone, but he eyes the label next to my piece and turns back to me.

He tilts his head and asks, "Are you the same Ms. Gray who made this?"

"Just Spencer, please. And yes, I am." I twist my hands together behind my back, hoping he can't tell how nervous I am to have my work on display.

Add in the fact that I'm sure dodging creepy men is going to be on my itinerary for the rest of the night and one could consider me an overstimulated ball of anxiety. I need him to stay. I need him to like my art. Then maybe Hugh will go away.

"You don't need this one, Anthony. I'm sure you can find another that will do just fine," Hugh argues.

"This one won't go in my stable. I think it'll satisfy my personal needs," Anthony answers resolutely.

Stable?

Anthony's gaze darts between me and the fired clay.

Is he shocked that I made it? Is that a good thing?

Staring at the piece he questions, "How old are you, Ms. Gray?"

"Seventeen," I reply automatically.

He takes a step closer and invades my space. "Tell me something, Ms. Gray. What do you feel when you look at this?"

His question throws me off balance. Art is emotion—I know that—but usually that's a question the viewer asks themselves, not the artist.

I attempt to ignore his proximity and turn to the sculpture. I dig deep and pull the feelings I felt when I saw that homeless man sitting in the cold. He looked as if he had given up.

My posture goes limp and my voice breaks. "Alone. Hopeless."

A hand sweeps my hair away from my shoulder, exposing my skin there. I gasp and am pulled back to the moment. Anthony's hand rests on my bare upper back as he pulls out his phone and begins to type. There's a chime before he stores his phone away.

Mom rushes over from the corner and places a sticker on the label, indicating the artwork has sold. I eye the label being discussed, and Mom shakes her head, indicating not to question it.

Mom puts on her best smile, and a light enters her face. "Congratulations, Mr. Cole. You've made a fine purchase."

"Indeed, I have, Mariana." His tone is smooth.

Where is the gallery owner?

My forehead scrunches, and Anthony smirks. It's like he can read my mind. One deep stare and he knows me.

I choose to voice my question anyway. "Where—"

Anthony interrupts me before I can finish. His eyes never leave mine, but his next comment is directed behind him. "Run along, Hugh. This one is mine."

CHAPTER 1

SPENCER

Handcuffs are not fun. Zero out of ten do not recommend.

Maybe if Zane put me in them with the intent to do other activities . . .

But no.

I'm handcuffed to a fucking bed that I slept in, alone. They didn't lock me in the room though—probably because the bed frame is solid. No matter how much I pull on my new steel jewelry, the headboard won't budge. It's like they nailed it into the wall.

It's only your right hand.

That's beside the point!

Fortunately, the room is comfortable. It has an urban look with an exposed brick accent wall, industrial pipes, dark wood used as shelves, and neutral linens. The bed is memory foam, and the temperature is cool enough at night that I actually need the blanket.

"Bathroom time, Mama," Rio says as he enters the room.

I sigh dramatically. "Finally."

Rio has come in a few times to let me pee, and thankfully, he lets me do that in private, unlike a certain friend of his. Zane brings me food—all my favorites—which only makes this situation more frustrating. I know none of the food they bring me is takeout because I can smell it cooking for an hour or so before it's brought to me, which means Asher makes it, but he has yet to come in the room.

"You've barely touched your water." Rio motions to the glass on the nightstand next to me, frowning at it.

"Yes, but now I get a break from staring at the wall." Sarcasm leaks through my tone.

Rio smirks. "We gave you the remote. You could watch TV."

"I don't want to watch TV. I want to go home."

"Which home would that be? The one in Chelsea, or the new one you were planning to make in California?"

Biting my lip, my eyes dart away. "I don't know what you're talking about." The sentence ends on a high pitch.

Rio reaches into his back pocket, pulls out a slip of paper, and reads, "Spencer Smith. Changing your name? It's not very original." He raises a brow at me then continues reading. "Departing Port Authority yesterday afternoon and arriving in Los Angeles, California tomorrow evening. Safe to say you missed your ride."

My stomach rolls. "Where did you find that?"

"Where do you think?"

I feel the color rise in my cheeks as I think of the things he probably found in my bag. "You had no right to go through my things."

Rio marches to the bed and leans over me, his face inches from mine. "I had every right. I told you to run to me, and you did."

"I was just checking—"

"You were going to leave, but you came here instead. I also found this little toy." He pulls out my waterproof green Rabbit vibrator.

A trapdoor opens in my belly, and my free hand darts out to grab the vibrator, but Rio moves it just out of reach. "Ah ah ah. If you really want it that bad, I can help you out, seeing how you're a bit tied up at the moment." He winks.

Not a bad idea.

Hell no!

He turns it over in his hands. "Where did you get this anyway? It's not very life-like. A little small."

Small? That thing is seven inches long! How is that small?!

"Oh my God! Just give it back!" I move for the vibrator again, but he holds it far enough away so I can't get it.

"No. I think I'll keep this safe for a little while longer." His lips are almost touching mine. If only he'd move a little closer.

Then an image flashes in my mind. The sight of Rio with a knife standing over two men tied to metal chairs.

I recoil from him, and a hard look crosses his face. "One day, you won't look at me like that."

"You hurt them."

"They were bad men and deserved what they got."

"How can you say that?"

"Easily." His voice is cold. "They're the ones who shot up Abstract Dreams. They're the ones who killed Lance."

I gasp, and the color leaves my face. Does that mean they found Pierce too? Where Pierce is, Anthony is not far behind. Just the thought of Anthony in the same vicinity as Rio, Zane, and Asher is going to make me break out in hives.

But I can't let Rio know anything is amiss . . .

I huff out a breath and attempt to cross my arms. A bit difficult when I have only one arm that can complete the motion.

"My friends are going to wonder where I am."

Rio shrugs. "I texted them and told them you're off finding inspiration for your exhibit."

I narrow my eyes at him. "I think I made it pretty clear that the exhibit is the last thing on my mind when I bought the damn bus ticket." I sit a little taller. "Besides, you don't have anyone's number."

"That's what you think," he scoffs. I raise an eyebrow in lieu of a verbal reply. "Okay, so I only have Hayes's digits, but I'll have everyone else's soon. They love me."

I don't like that he's right; all of my friends practically eat out of the palm of his hand.

"But that's a nonissue because I didn't use my phone. I used yours."

"What!?" My eyes blink incredulously.

"You really should change your password on that thing. Zero-six-one-one? The day we met? Really?"

My nose scrunches, and my eyes squint as I attempt to do the math in my head, but I end up with a headache instead. "That's not the day we met."

"True, but don't worry, I took care of that for you."

Fucking hell. Now I'm going to have to figure out the day we met, which is in my calendar . . . in my phone, which I don't have, and is now locked with a new password.

I roll my eyes at him and imagine punching him in the arm. I know it's a bit juvenile, but there's not much else I can do with literally one hand tied to the damn headboard.

Rio pulls out my phone from his other back pocket.

What else is he hiding back there?

"Speaking of your phone . . ." He rolls my phone around in his hands while he chooses his words carefully. "You didn't tell me about the texts."

Playing dumb has become my new m.o. so why give up now?

"What texts?"

"You know what texts I'm talking about. The ones from Anthony."

I turn a cold eye on him. "Yes, I did. You're my lawyer, remember?"

"I mean the last few you've gotten. Why didn't you tell me?"

My lips roll inward as I keep my answer to myself. He won't like what I have to say, especially after all three of them ganged up on me when Asher caught me trying to flee my apartment after the whole sand fiasco.

Yeah, that made it perfectly clear they're a smidge overprotective.

Rio narrows his eyes, lets out a frustrated sigh, and releases me from the cuffs with a key. He gently massages my red wrist, and I don't like how the action causes a fluttering in my belly. I'm not supposed to be yearning for his touch. I'm supposed to be trying to get away—far away.

He must see the indecision in my eyes because he leans back in. Right when I think he's about to go for a repeat performance of our studio escapades, he lifts me to my feet and leads me to the en suite.

I wish I could report that the peeing chases away this aching need, but that's not the case. I only get a temporary reprieve.

The thought of Rio, Zane, and Asher being complicit and actively participating in the death of those men terrifies me. I know what I saw; those images aren't going away anytime soon. But burying my head in the sand isn't an option here.

So why don't those images do anything to kill my desire for my men?

CHAPTER 2

ZANE

"This is not how I saw Spencer moving in with us."
Rio shakes his head.

"You're shitting me, right?" Asher snaps.

"Did I stutter, *hombre*?"

Asher has been acting like we shoved a cactus up his ass. I don't see what his problem is. Eventually, Spencer would've ended up right where she is now.

My bed.

How she got there wasn't ideal, but when Asher called Rio and me after Gabriel shot his homeboys, I didn't expect to see Spencer there. My first instinct was to get her as far away from the MS-13 as possible. I wasn't going to let those three, especially not fucking Gabriel Castillo, lay eyes on my Angel. I needed to know she would be safe.

Naturally, the safest place she could be is in my bed.

Asher punches Rio in the arm, bringing me back to the problem at hand. Rio's mom, Paloma, called and said that she expects us all to be at family dinner tomorrow night. We've been sitting around our modest kitchen table, brainstorming what to do.

"We can't go. We'll all just stay home and tell her we're sick." Asher leans back in his chair and crosses his arms.

Rio gives Asher an implacable expression. "You know that won't work. My mom will come by and check."

One time, when we were all in college, we were swamped with essays, exams, and—in all honesty—were a bit hungover. We told Rio's mom we weren't coming to the house for Sunday dinner because we were sick. Not even a few hours later, Paloma showed up at our college dorm, ordered us into bed, and wouldn't leave until late that night. She took our temperatures, rubbed a homemade salve on our chests, and made us homemade chicken noodle soup. There is no saying "no" to Paloma Flores.

"Okay, so one of us will pretend to be sick and stay with Spencer while the other two go." Asher throws his hands in the air.

I chime in before Asher can delude himself further. "We know what we have to do."

Asher groans and drags a hand down his face while Rio sits, seemingly unbothered.

"She won't go for it," Asher states.

"Yeah, if *you* ask her." Rio chuckles.

"She's not happy with *you* either," Asher snaps back.

"I'll do it." I stand from my chair as Rio protests.

"What? I wanted to call dibs. Not cool." Rio hangs his head like I kicked his nonexistent puppy.

I ignore Asher's protests, grab the rabbit food pizza, and trudge up the wooden stairs. Spencer's look of horror after Asher found her flashes through my mind. She looked at me like she was afraid of me. She should be afraid, but not because of me.

Never because of me.

My free hand rests on the frame as I stare at the door as if I'll magically get X-ray vision and I can see through the wood and straight to Spencer.

I've been in a few times, but she's given me the silent treatment so far. I won't pretend it doesn't hurt, but I can be strong for her. I'll take her anger for now.

Her heart is made of gold, and she won't be able to stay mad at me for long.

Fortifying my heart, I enter the room, and Spencer's eyes snap to mine. Once again, she doesn't say anything, but that's okay. I'm a patient man.

I set the pizza next to her, wait at the foot of my bed, and let the silence around us settle.

She does her best to ignore the cheesy goodness, but she's practically salivating. She opens the box and takes a bite with her non-cuffed hand.

I used to think Sal's Pizza could cure anything, but Spencer is determined to hold on to her resentment. She takes delicate, small bites and scooches as far away from me as possible.

Watching her eat and knowing it's going to fill out her hips and ass even more makes me hard. I'll have more to grab on to when I slam into her from behind and watch her ass bounce with each drive of my hips.

She finishes off a slice, and her eyes take me in. Her nostrils flare at my calm exterior. Little does she know, I'm ready to burst out of my skin. I'm desperate to touch her. Patience is my strong suit, but she seems to know how to test that damn strength without even trying.

Spencer is laid out on *my* bed like a fucking feast. Her hair hangs in its natural waves over one shoulder. A pair of skintight workout shorts hug her curves, and an oversized tee does little to hide the swell of her breasts.

She finally cracks when she spits her question out at me. "Is there a reason you're still in here?"

I don't give her an answer, and her mouth tightens into a stubborn line.

She'll crack any moment now.

Three, two . . .

"If you're just going to stare at me, you can leave. I have nothing to say to you—nothing to offer you," Spencer snaps.

A smirk tugs at the corner of my mouth. "We both know that's not true, Angel. There's plenty you could offer that I would gladly take because, when it comes to you, I can never get enough."

If her rapid breathing didn't give away how she feels, then the squirming does. She wants me. She just doesn't *want* to want me.

But she does.

Her irritation sets in as she frowns and raises her voice. "Why are you here? If it's just to torture me, then leave. You guys think you have the right to just do whatever the fuck you want? You handcuff me to the bed, you take my phone, and you all walk around all sexy, like it's your job to look like sex on a stick! And I just have to lay here and do nothing? It's infuriating!"

"Well, I think I have a right to be in my own room," I say with a confident shrug and stalk towards her.

Spencer gasps, seemingly panicked, as her eyes go wide and lock with mine.

"What did you think? That we just had an extra room?" I lean over her and place one knee on the bed next to her hip. I raise my brows at her condescendingly to get a reaction, and man, does she react.

"I want to go to a different room!" If she was standing, she'd be stomping her foot.

Goading her shouldn't be the goal, but this is the first time she's talked to me in forty-eight hours. I'll take whatever words of hers I can get.

I need them.

I chuckle, placing my hands on either side of her hips as she sits up straight with her one hand secured to my headboard. I lower until my mouth is almost touching hers. "You want to go to Asher's room?"

"No." She clenches her jaw, and a vein in her temple pulses.

Button pushed.

Her cheeks turn a bright red as I lower my body and align my dick with her pussy.

My voice drops to let her know how serious I am. "Like hell will I ever let you out of this room, let alone this bed, while you're in danger. Especially not when you're lying here like you've been waiting for me, all day, to come home and fuck you."

"Oh, please. No need to turn into a caveman." She attempts to sound indignant, but her words come out breathy.

"I will never take chances when it comes to your safety."

She turns her head to avoid the intensity in my eyes, but I want her eyes on me, drinking me in. I need her just as obsessed with me as I am with her.

"Tell me something, Angel. Are you wet?"

"What?"

"Do you think I didn't notice how you squeezed these sexy thighs when I walked in? How your pulse increased when I stood over you?" I rock my hips forward. When she feels how hard I am, she moans.

"I don't want this."

"Don't want this, or don't want to admit how much you want this?"

She opens her mouth, and I cut her off before she can speak. "Don't lie, Spencer. I know when you're lying."

"No, you don't!" she protests and then looks me right in the eye. "I. Don't. Want. This." But her gaze darts to the left for a split second.

"Lie," I growl. Sitting up, I yank her shorts off. She fights me, but her struggle just makes it easier. She's wearing a simple white thong and right in the middle, there's a wet spot.

"Lie to me again, Angel. Try it. Tell me how you don't want my fat cock thrusting into your pussy until you come, screaming my name."

Her nostrils flare and her free hand grips the sheets, but she doesn't deny it.

Finally.

Dipping my head, I drag my nose across her covered pussy and breathe her in. "Heaven. You smell like heaven. Just like I knew you would."

Hooking my fingers in her thong, I drag it down her long legs. Tossing it to the side, I run my hands up her inner thighs. She parts for me without protest. I kiss and suck the skin on her inner thighs as I make my way upward.

Just her smell and the little noises she's making almost have me coming in my jeans. It takes all my willpower to hold it back.

I knew I'd get to this point with Spencer one day, but I was not prepared. Her glistening pussy is more beautiful than I imagined.

With my face right at the juncture of her thighs, I look up at Spencer. "Last chance, Angel. Tell me 'No.'"

Instead of answering, she bites her bottom lip and her hips lift off the mattress, barely an inch, offering her sweet slit to me.

Don't need to tell me twice.

Without hesitation, I tilt my head down and lick her, entrance to clit, then swirl my tongue around her nub. The honey taste that is wholly Spencer explodes in my mouth.

And just like that, I'm addicted.

Spencer moans and lightly lifts her hips, pushing my face back into her pussy.

Give me a Change-of-Address form because I live here now. I'll happily make her come like this at least three times a day, every day.

Probably more.

"Hands on the headboard, Angel, and hold on."

She whimpers at my command and complies. Her hands go above her head, and she grips the headboard. Her knuckles turn white from the intensity.

My next lick earns me a gasp from her beautiful throat. I can't wait to wrap my hand around it as I thrust into her.

I get lost in her sounds as I attack her core with my tongue. Once she's soaking the sheet underneath, I circle her clit and tease her opening with my finger, but I don't push inside. I continue stroking her entrance, and more whimpers pour from her.

Then I finally get what I've been wanting.

"Please, Zane. Oh God, please."

"Please, what, Spencer?"

She lets out a frustrated sound. "I need you inside me!"

Smirking, I reply, "If that's what you really want." Her arousal gathers on my fingers, and I use it to push two into her pussy.

"Oh shit! Yes!" Spencer exclaims. I'm sure the neighbors can hear her by now.

My tongue flicks her clit repeatedly as I thrust my fingers in and out of her, driving her wild. Her hips find a rhythm, adding to her pleasure.

Her panting increases, but it's not enough. I need her completely undone for me.

I cover her bundle of nerves with my mouth and suck. Her inner muscles contract around my fingers, and my hand floods with her cum. Pleasure overtakes her face as she shouts, "Zane!"

Hearing my name on her lips, knowing I'm the one who turned her into this wanton creature . . .

I'm the one undone.

My fingers continue working her pussy as I watch her climax fade. Pulling my fingers from her, I sit up on my knees and undo my pants. I push them down my thighs, along with my boxers, and my cock springs free.

Spencer tracks my movements with hunger in her eyes. Her tongue darts out, and she licks her lips as she stares at my thick length.

"Watch me, baby." My drenched hand circles my erect cock and coats the smooth skin in her cum. I use her release as a lubricant and pump my shaft a few times. Her desire peaks again as she observes my movements. She attempts to squeeze her thighs together, but my frame is in the way.

"Tell me you don't want me inside you, Angel. Tell me you don't want me to shove my fat cock in your cunt and make you come again."

Color rises in her cheeks as she, once again, gives me what I need. "Please."

Digging in my pocket, I pull out the key and unlock the secured cuff. "Sit up and hands behind your back."

She follows my orders swiftly, and I cuff her hands together behind her back. I grab her by the hips, lift, and then slowly lower her, impaling her on my stiff length, inch by inch. She cries out as I groan. Her muscles flutter, causing my dick to twitch inside her. Even though I just worked her with my hand, she's tight as hell, and her cunt is stretched seductively around me.

She's so warm. So wet.

"Condom?"

"I can't leave your perfect pussy now that I know how you feel squeezing my dick," I growl against her lips. "I'm clean. I promise." I've never taken a woman bare before.

"It's okay," she pants against me, "I have an implant in my arm. We're good."

Fuck. This is perfect. *She's* perfect.

Lifting her off my lap, I drop her back down and thrust up at the same time. We groan together. "Tell me we get to be like this every time. Nothing between us."

"Yes, yes, yes."

"Such a good girl." When I give her praise, her pussy chokes my cock, stealing my breath. "Now, bounce on Daddy's lap until you soak my dick with your cum."

We continue our motions. Spencer bucking and swiveling her hips while I piston up into her. The sounds of our arousal echo in the room as my dick slides in and out of her swollen core.

I cover her mouth with mine, our lips and tongues dancing together. I want to swallow all of her beautiful sounds. My hands find her perfect breasts and lightly pinch her hardened tips.

When I pinch harder, her toes curl, and she screams into my mouth. Her pussy contracts, triggering my own release. Ecstasy floods my body as my seed spills inside her and Spencer milks every drop from me.

Once we've both come down from the high, our kiss turns lazy as my hands travel up into her hair. I massage her scalp as she continues to relax in my arms, and I unlock the cuffs. I lay her on her back, then massage her wrists, kissing the inside of each.

"You're everything to me," I confess, and tears line her eyes.

Pulling out, I glance down and watch my cum trickle from her core. And just like that, I'm ready to go again, but she needs time to recover. She's going to be sore.

Spencer squeals and tries to snap her legs closed. "Don't look!"

"Why not?"

"It's weird!"

Holy hell. This woman is adorable.

"I think it's fucking hot."

Her brows pinch together, and she blinks rapidly.

"Trust me, Angel."

She eyes me skeptically but finally relents. "I do."

The air in my lungs vanishes. Her trust is everything.

Climbing off the bed, I clean up in my bathroom and wet a soft washcloth in the sink. When I return, Spencer is drifting off to sleep. The cold from the towel makes her jolt. With my hand in the center of her chest, I ease her back down.

She squeaks when I run the fabric down her slit again, and she covers her face with her hands. "This is so weird."

"What is?" I know what she's talking about, but I want to hear her say it.

"Oh my God. You're literally cleaning my vagina."

I shrug. "It's my mess."

"This is still weird."

"Angel, I had my tongue, fingers, and dick in your pussy. I bound your hands behind your back. I *should* take care of you, and you should expect it."

I don't want to think about the one that came before and the lack of aftercare. If I go there, I'll need to kill him right now with my bare fucking hands.

Once Spencer is clean, I grab a bottle of massage oil from my nightstand. "Roll over."

"What? Why?"

"Just do it."

She shakes her head but does as I ask.

I pour a generous amount into my hands and knead the muscles in her back. My hands glide over her smooth skin. I find the knots along her shoulders and neck and rub each one until her entire body loses its tension.

Spencer groans. "Fuck, Zane. That feels so good."

"Keep talking like that, and I'll do you again right now. I need to let you rest, but I only have so much control when it comes to you."

Spencer gasps but remains quiet for the rest of her massage. Once her muscles are loose, I lie next to her, on my side, and adjust her body so her back is plastered to my front.

"Why the handcuffs?"

Her question catches me off guard. I shouldn't be surprised; I highly doubt she's ever done anything like that. I should have talked to her about it before just going with it.

But as much as I want to give her everything, there are some memories that are too painful to revisit. And if I'm going to share with her, I need her to share with me. "Why does Anthony scare you?"

Her shoulders tense, but not a word leaves her lips.

Before I close my eyes, I give Spencer the news I was supposed to. "Paloma wants us to come for dinner."

She twists so her face is in mine. "Who the hell is Paloma?"

The jealousy radiating from her fills my heart.

Yeah, she wants me.

I hold back a laugh and answer, "Rio's mother."

"Oh."

"Yeah. *Oh.*"

"We're going tomorrow and you're coming with."

A mischievous glint enters her eye.

Before she can put together any ridiculous plans, I inform her, "I should mention that Paloma knows what we do and who we are. She trusts us. If you try to tell her you've been chained to my bed, she's not going to call the cops."

"Fucking perfect," she murmurs as she turns back over.

I'm going to hell, that's for sure—my ticket was signed years ago—so telling a small fib isn't going to make it any worse. Paloma kind of knows what we do. She was there for Rio during all the shit that went down with Izzy. She won't call the cops, but she might rip us all new ass holes.

"Sleep, Angel." I run my fingers through her hair and gently work out each tangle.

After little snores begin coming out of Spencer, I let myself dream.

I dream of a world where we all live together under one roof. Spencer is safe, there are no human traffickers to kill, and we get to lie like this in bed most days.

Something moves in my heart, and determination takes hold of me.

This will be our life. I'll make sure of it.

CHAPTER 3

SPENCER

My sexcapades with Zane have left me torn. Obviously, I enjoyed the hell out of it, but shouldn't I be mad at him? Can I be mad and still want him at the same time? The back and forth is giving me a headache. To be fair, what was I supposed to do when he took my shorts off? My body had a mind of its own and then his tongue . . .

Oh God. His tongue.

Now I'm taking an extra-long shower, and I hope I use all the hot water.

Petty? Yes.

Do I care? No.

I've been handcuffed to a bed so they can deal with cold showers. I don't care that the handcuffs may have been fun in the end. I stand by the principle that you don't handcuff someone you claim is your girlfriend to your bed without her permission.

Once the water starts to decline from scorching hot to luke-warm, I deem my mission accomplished and towel myself off.

Before Zane left to give me privacy, he said my clothes

were in the closet. Opening the doors, I first dig to find my duffle bag and check to make sure I still have Abuela's urn. As my hand finds the cool ceramic, I'm able to breathe easily again.

Stepping back, I focus on getting dressed, but the plethora of women's clothing pulls me up short. The clothes I packed are here and displayed on hangers, but there's more than just my clothes.

There are women's clothes that are most definitely not mine.

Am I expected to wear the clothes of their previous hook-ups? Are they fucking kidding? Is this another one of those times I think they're joking but then it turns out they actually aren't?

If I had matches, I'd set the lot on fire and watch it burn. They want it to be this way? Fine. I can play.

I refuse to touch the other clothes even though I'm tempted when I spot a tank top that looks soft—it would hang on my frame perfectly.

Fuck that perfect material. Not happening.

I reach for a pair of jeans and a simple scoop-neck tee that I know are mine. I don't need *those* clothes to feel confident.

After a quick swipe of makeup and styling my hair, I'm ready to go.

WE CRAM into Zane's clown car, and thank God, I'm sans handcuffs. Although Zane made a show of putting them in his pocket, letting me know that he has them on hand if I misbehave.

His words, not mine.

Just seeing the handcuffs had my heartbeat picking up and

an ache forming between my legs. But the feeling diminished as soon as Asher came into view.

Asher still isn't speaking to me even while he's jammed into the seat next to me. I guess we're playing the quiet game again. The asshole didn't even visit me in my prison cell—also known as Zane's bedroom.

Rio is acting like this is a normal Sunday, as if we do this all the time.

Me? I'm freaking the fuck out.

It's not like I found the men I'm falling for torturing a couple of guys in their basement.

Was. *Was* falling for.

Gotta keep that straight in my head.

But two of the three did give you the best orgasms of your life . . .

Ugh.

"You'll love Carmen. Ignore Elena and Mariela when they start in on each other, and Solana may not talk much. My mom may seem like a lot at first, but you'll get used to it. She likes to make sure we're taken care of, so we'll probably be taking half of the leftovers home with us." You'd think it was his birthday or something with how he's practically bouncing in his seat.

I blink at Rio's enthusiasm and the fact that this man has four sisters. Four. One, two, three, four. Four! I'm an only child, but holy shit!

Dear God, please don't make them mean sisters. I'm already confused enough as it is about all this shit.

My eyes wander to Asher. He's staring out the window, and it takes more effort than I care to admit to not take it personally. Maybe he just likes the scenery and isn't purposefully keeping his attention as far away from me as possible.

But the probability of that is low.

His disinterest only fuels the anger that started when I looked in Zane's fucking closet.

Fuck these guys.

I mean, you've already fucked one of them.

I internally roll my eyes at the annoying voice in my head that may or may not be correct.

The rest of the drive goes by in silence except for the Latin Pop music lightly streaming from the speakers. Rio had won control of the music in a game of rock, paper, scissors with Zane.

We come to a stop in front of a modest, two-story home with light gray vinyl siding and white shutters. A short, chain link fence marks the property lines, and a few simple brown brick steps lead to the front door. The rose bushes along the fence give the home an extra touch of welcome. I imagine a little Rio with dark hair running around the small front lawn, giving his mother grief and laughing while he does it. I smile at the image.

"I love it when you smile like that, Angel."

A frown immediately takes over my face, but my protest has the opposite effect when Rio and Zane chuckle. Even Asher is smirking.

Fucking men.

I lean back in my seat, fold my arms over my chest, and ignore the idiots around me.

While I'm stewing in my anger, my door opens, and I'm hauled into a warm firm chest. Horny Spencer swoons, but I keep a scowl on my face even though I'm dying to lean into the solid body. But when I glance up and see blond hair, it's not that hard to keep the scowl in place.

Asher doesn't let me pull away. "Calm down, Princess."

With a tight expression, I retort, "Don't you know not to tell a woman to calm down? She will always do the opposite."

The challenging look Asher gives me would probably terrify me if I didn't know him better. But I do know him . . . kind of.

Either way, his "I'm a badass FBI agent" face doesn't make me cower.

"*Vamos, tórtolos,*" Rio says in jest. *Come on, lovers.* "If we don't go inside, my mom will come out looking for us."

Another tug and I'm free, but my breath hitches at the loss of his warmth. I follow Rio and Asher up the front steps with Zane trailing behind me. Nice and secure between my captors—also known as my boyfriends—where I'm sure they'll keep me for the foreseeable future.

When we enter the house I'm overwhelmed with smells of cilantro, cumin, and chili powder. Tears threaten to make an appearance as I'm assaulted with a flood of memories of Abuela making dishes like pozole and chicken enchiladas. I keep my head down, eyes glued to the light wood flooring, hoping no one will notice, because this is not how I want to be introduced to Rio's family.

Talk about embarrassing.

Before we get through the entryway, Zane snags my hand in a gentle grasp and spins me around. I don't flinch or try to yank away as he checks me over from my glossy eyes to my sneakers. I don't know what he's searching for, but it's like he gives my heart a hard tug with his attention.

Zane reaches a hand to my face and cradles my cheek in his palm. "Don't cry, Angel. Everything will be okay. I've got you. You're safe."

I don't like that he always knows what I need and what to say to make me want to jump into his arms. But then I remember what I found in his closet, and the moment abruptly ends.

Zane's brows pull together, and his head tilts to the side. "What—"

"Don't," I cut him off in a firm tone and stomp away in the direction I think Asher and Rio went.

I find myself in a simple, updated kitchen with white and gray marble countertops, light gray cabinetry, and signs that say things like "Kiss the Cook," "I Can Fix Anything but Stupid," and "Made With Love." A golden oak table sits by the back window, with matching chairs surrounding it.

Rio stands at the stove, tying on a simple apron. But the words on it are not simple and not what I was expecting. It reads, "Once you put my meat in your mouth, you're gonna want to swallow," with a picture of a steak at the bottom.

I belt out a laugh, and Rio laughs along with me. "I'm so happy you like it."

"You keep this here, at your mom's house?"

"What do you mean? I brought it with me."

I compose myself as the reminder that I'm supposed to be pissed pops into my head. If it's going to be this difficult to stay mad at them about the damn clothes, how am I going to fare when it comes to the dead bodies in the basement? Literally. I'd like to think I'm able to hold my ground, but I can't help how my body responds to each of these men. The constant turmoil in my chest subsides, and peace spreads to every limb.

Zane enters the room and responds before I can. "Your mom is going to freak when she sees you wearing that again."

"Nah," Rio counters, but doubt enters his face.

"Rio, *mi hijo*! You better not be burning my *caldo de pollo*!" A voice booms from upstairs.

Rio smirks, rolls his eyes, and turns back to the pot. Zane moves past me, grabs a stack of plates from an upper cabinet, and heads for the back door of the kitchen.

Each of these men works seamlessly together.

They want me here, but I'm not sure what my role is.

My feet shuffle side to side. "Umm. Is there anything I can do to help?"

Rio turns off the burner and grabs a set of pot holders.

"You're good, Mama. The *caldo de pollo* is finished so we can take it outside. Hold the door for me?"

"Uh. Yeah, sure." Clumsily yanking the door open, I allow him to pass by.

The easy nature with which Rio navigates this fucking hornet's nest makes me envy his optimistic disposition. I wish I could be the same way.

Optimism shouldn't be expected of someone who recently caught their boyfriends torturing two guys . . . right?

Did I ever really accept the title they gave themselves in my hospital room?

Well, you were ready for another round with Zane. The same will probably be true of Rio.

Oh, fucking hell. Not now, Horny Spencer.

The backyard of the Flores home is as cozy as the rest of the home. It's well taken care of with trimmed grass, maintained bushes, and a few potted plants that look like they contain herbs. There are a couple of picnic tables that have been pushed together to make one long table, and it's surrounded by mismatched chairs, giving the whole setup a homely feel. The table is covered in a mountain of food.

I don't think I've even seen this much food at a buffet.

A few of the chairs are occupied by women who all look like they're related to Rio. They all have the same eyes, hair color, and nose.

One looks to be in her teens and her face is buried in a book as she sits curled in a ball in a white lawn chair. Her long, dark hair is braided to one side and rests over her shoulder.

Another looks like a young adult with enough moxie for everyone in the room as she types away on her phone. Her hair is curly and wild in a gorgeous, "I just came off the runway," kind of way. She's sitting opposite the first girl, and her breasts look ready to spill out of her top while her skirt looks like one little breeze will give everyone a show we didn't ask for.

Power to her. Wear what you want, honey.

The last of the unknown women scurries around the table and adjusts all the bowls and platters of food, muttering to herself about flow and space. Her hair is cropped short and a pair of simple glasses rest on the end of her nose. She has an air of maturity and superiority around her. An aura that screams, "You better do what I say, or there will be hell to pay."

Zane shuffles his way around the table setting the plates down while Asher sits in a chair at the far end, glowering at his phone.

Then it hits me. I'm about to meet his family and I have to pretend as if everything is normal.

Shit. Do I want them to like me? Do I even care? If I care, does that mean I want things to work out with my murderous boyfriends?

Fucking hell. I was not ready to answer the questions swirling around in my head.

The backdoor swings open, and out walks, who I assume is, Rio's mom. She's an older, short woman with long, curly hair streaked with gray. She's wearing jeans and a white tee covered by a plaid, floral, embroidered apron. The wrinkles around her eyes and the corners of her mouth are light and endearing.

"My boys!" she shouts and holds her arms wide.

Zane, Asher, and Rio stop what they're doing and make their way to her as if this is routine. She hugs and gives each of them a peck on the cheek, leaving behind a pink lip print. Asher wipes his away immediately, Rio makes a fuss that's clearly fake about his mom's kiss, and Zane beams at the show of love and slowly cleans off the lipstick.

This really is a home filled with love.

My mother loves me, I know that, but she showed it differently. She was what people would call a "helicopter mom." She was a bit emotionally distant, but she hovered. She always wanted to be involved, know where I was going, who I was with, and how long I'd be gone. She was protective and worried, but she didn't support my art until I was almost done with high school, when I finally sold my first sculpture.

Rio's mom seems to take a different approach to parenting. She appears to shower her kids, even those that aren't her own, with love—a lot of love. My mom doesn't hug me when I get home or kiss my cheek, but I know she cares. She just shows it in her own way.

Rio's mother's eyes connect with mine. She frowns and she smacks each of the guys upside the head.

Oh shit. Am I supposed to be here?

Rio rubs the back of his head. "Ouch, Ma! *¿Y por qué fue eso?*" *What was that for?*

"You didn't tell me you were bringing a girl! I would have dressed nicer!" She chastises them as she smooths out the wrinkles in her apron.

"You look great, Paloma," Zane reassures her.

I fiddle with my hair and bite the inside of my cheek as Rio places an arm around his mother and leads her over to me. "Má, *we* would like you to meet Spencer. She's the one who has been teaching me pottery. Spencer, this is my mother, Paloma."

Paloma raises her brows when he drops the "we" and I cringe, waiting for the judgment that never comes.

Turning on my southern charm, I extend my hand. "It's nice to meet you, Mrs. Flores."

She ignores my hand, steps forward, and wraps me in a warm embrace. She pours her maternal love through our brief physical connection, and once again, I hold back tears. The only other person to hug me this way died three years ago. I didn't realize how much I've missed Abuela's hugs until now.

"We hug here. I'm so happy I get to meet you. I've heard a lot about you."

My eyes almost pop out of my head as I look to Rio over Paloma's shoulder. He smirks and shrugs guiltlessly then nods towards Zane whose cheeks turn a little pink.

"Y'all talk about me?"

Zane nods while Rio blurts out, "Of course I do, Mama."

During all of this Asher hangs back, refusing to be part of the exchange as if he doesn't want to be associated with me at all. The thought stings, but I'm a big girl.

He wants to be an ass? Fine. He can be an ass. I'll do the same.

When Paloma and I part, Rio says, "Spencer moved in."

If I was drinking something, it'd be all over everyone right now.

I can't believe he just said that.

"No—I—It's not—"

Paloma's smile brightens her face even more. "A whirlwind romance. How beautiful," she comments wistfully.

Is this real life? Someone pinch me. What planet are these people from? How can they accept a relationship, *that I'm not even sure is happening,* like this so easily?

Everyone ignores my shock, and I'm led over to the other three women by Paloma with Zane, Rio, and Asher trailing behind. "Come meet Rio's sisters."

"Where's Carmen?" Rio questions with a hint of worry as he scans the yard, even though he knows she's not here.

Paloma waves off his concern. "She'll be here soon, don't worry. She had a test to study for."

"Spencer, this is Elena." Paloma gestures to the sister with short hair. "And Mariela." The one with the club clothing. "And Solana." The sister with braided hair and a book.

My weight shifts side to side and a tingling sensation sweeps up the back of my neck as I remember where I've heard the name "Solana" before.

Well, I feel stupid.

I glance over at Zane, and he gives me an easy smile that says he knows what I'm thinking of.

"Hi! It's nice to meet y'all." I give a small wave.

Solana gives a small smile and returns to her book, *Breaking Dawn*.

"Y'all?" Mariela snickers.

My cheeks pinken slightly. I haven't been mocked for my southern drawl in years. The first time I said "Y'all" in front of Hayes, he thought I was being sarcastic. I quickly realized my Southern slang would give away my roots, and I couldn't have that. So, I stopped saying things like "Bless your heart," but I have never been able to shake "Y'all."

"Mariela! Manners," Paloma scolds.

Elena gives Mariela a pinch on her arm.

"Ow! What the fuck!?" Mariela rubs her tender skin.

Elena doesn't look remorseful. "You don't have to be a bitch. Rio's never brought anyone home."

Wait. Never?

Then she turns to me and gives a quick smile. "It's great to have you here."

"Thanks! Dinner looks delicious. I don't get home-cooked meals often."

Mariela rolls her eyes and goes back to scrolling on her phone.

"Ignore her. She isn't out of her teenage phase." Elena comforts me after Mariela's dismissal and I try to not to stress over Mariela's obvious dislike.

Do I want their approval? If I do, does that mean I want *them*? Can I live with knowing what they've done and, what I assume, they regularly do?

While I debate over my little existential crisis, Elena leads me into a chair in the middle of the table, and Asher plants his grumpy ass in the seat right next to me. My heart equally warms and stirs. Rio claims the seat on my other side and gives Asher a stern look while Zane looks at us with his lips turned up in a soft smile.

What the hell is going on with these three?

As I'm consulting my manual, *How to Decipher the Grunts and Gestures of Cavemen*, the back door bangs open, and another woman with long, dark, curly hair comes through in a hurry. She's in gray sweats and a cropped NYU T-shirt and has a frantic energy about her.

"I'm here! Sorry I'm late!"

"That's Carmen. She's studying to be a lawyer like Rio," Elena whispers to me and my heart warms at the idea of Rio's sister following in his footsteps.

Okay, maybe not all *of his footsteps.*

Carmen rushes over to Rio and hurries out an unsolicited explanation. "I didn't invite them. I swear it, Rio. I didn't."

Rio, Asher, and Zane's faces go hard while I tilt my head to the side and blink. Asher stands, pulling me with him and positions his large body between the door and me. Rio reaches under his shirt and pulls out a knife in each hand and faces the back door as well. Guns suddenly appear in Zane and Asher's hands.

Are we preparing for the apocalypse or something?

When the door swings open again, three, tattooed, bronze-skinned men walk through, and I recognize them immediately. My whole body locks up and a cold sweat breaks out on my neck even though the New York heat hangs in the air.

With arms open wide the one in the middle says, "*!Hola, Mamá Flores! ¿Qué pasa?*"

Zane growls. "Oh, fuck no."

CHAPTER 4

ASHER

These fuckers, really? It's bad enough that we run into them during investigations, but here at Paloma's? Fuck that.

"Put those things away, *mis hijos*!"

Paloma has a rule: No weapons at dinner. But I'm always packing when I leave the house.

One time, I was approached on the street outside of work hours by the spouse of someone I had arrested the day before. She brought a gun and was waving it around. She just wanted her wife to come home, but that's not going to happen for at least five more years—I collared the right suspect.

But I understand desperation. When you have a father like the one I did, desperation becomes your companion.

Paloma swatting at my arm brings me back to the present, and I reluctantly put my gun away in the holster at the back of my pants. Zane does the same, and Rio slips his knife in its sheath.

Gabriel, Mateo, and Diego approach like we're not a threat to them.

Fucking idiots.

Paloma kisses each of them on the cheek in greeting. Elena folds her arms across her chest and heads back inside—no doubt going to get more place settings for the extra guests. Mariela doesn't look up from her phone, and Solana is still glued to her book.

Apparently, vampires and werewolves are more captivating than a possible gunfight in her backyard.

Carmen is standing next to Rio with her fists balled at her sides. If looks could kill, those three gangbangers would be dead ten times over right now. She looks even more pissed than Zane, Rio, and I combined.

"I told you not to come," she hisses.

Gabriel cocks his head to the side. "Is that what you said when you left my house this morning?"

"When you what!?" Rio shouts.

"Don't make this into something it's not, and not in front of the family," Carmen grits out.

Diego looks on and keeps his facial features blank. Mateo looks a little too invested in the exchange between Carmen and Gabriel.

When Diego's eyes finally connect with Carmen's, there's a longing there that can't be hidden. Then I notice the heat in Mateo's gaze and the way Gabriel is unabashedly undressing Carmen with his eyes.

Shit. This is not going to go well.

Rio comes to the same conclusion a second after I do, and he launches himself at all three men.

"You *hijos de putas*! That's my fucking sister!"

Paloma throws her hands up in exasperation. *"Ay dios mío."*

Rio is taking on all three guys like a pro, and Zane rushes in to help, fists swinging. Zane has always been someone who likes things to be fair.

There's a touch on my arm and when I glance down I see Spencer peeking around my large frame. She clutches me in a strangling grip and pulls me closer.

Yes, Baby. Need me.

"They won't touch you, Princess."

"I know." Her whispered words are a punch to the gut—the truth behind them, pure. I can't give into the temptation, but the way I want Spencer should be illegal.

"As you should," I reply with a smirk. I shouldn't flirt, but I need the fear in her eyes to disappear.

She sighs and shakes her head at me, causing her beautiful, flowy hair to sway. What I wouldn't give to run my fingers through her hair as she shouts my name, again.

"What the fuck is going on here!" Elena is standing on the doorstep with plates, cups, and utensils stacked in her arms.

"Language, *mija!*"

The fighting pauses as each man turns towards Elena. "This isn't a bar brawl! Get yourselves together. God! *Actúan como niños,*" Elena chastises. *You're acting like children.*

"But—" Rio stammers.

"Nuh uh. *No quiero escucharlos*"—*I don't want to hear it*—"I don't care what they did—suck it up for the next few hours. You're stressing out Mom. You know her heart can't handle another trip to the hospital."

Elena's reminder of Paloma's heart attack makes everyone wince.

Paloma claps her hands together. "New rule: No fists at dinner. Next person to pull a gun or take a swing has to clean up dinner."

Zane huffs and crosses his arms; Gabriel, Mateo, and Diego shrug in agreement. Not that they could battle it out against Paloma anyway.

Paloma takes charge again, ordering everyone to their seats.

I tug Spencer back down into the chair next to me when she tries to step away and take a different seat.

Not happening, Princess.

She gave me her trust. I may not allow myself to touch her the way I'm desperate to, but I'll keep her safe no matter what it takes.

She shoots a glare laced with confusion my way while my face remains empty. She can't know she's my every thought, my every desire. Because she *can't* be those things to me.

This woman has the ability to ruin what we've built. Rachel almost did it once, but Spencer has the power to break us irrevocably.

CHAPTER 5

SPENCER

’m ashamed to admit that the neanderthal display of physical prowess almost had me opening my legs in invitation. Seeing Rio take on three grown men by himself was reckless, and I shouldn't encourage that kind of behavior, but then Zane jumped into the fray, and I couldn't stop the pulsing need between my thighs.

Fucking Horny Spencer!

If we weren't with Rio's family, I would have offered myself up for the main course, regardless of the fact that I'm mad at them.

I have needs too.

The three men who crashed dinner terrify me, but with my men close, I know I'm safe. From what I've gathered, their names are Gabriel, Mateo, and Diego, they might have a thing with Carmen, and they're unfazed when murdering men in basements.

Then the cold bucket of water that is Asher Dawson was thrown onto my hormones when he made me sit next to him. I wish I could say that I don't long for him to call me

"Princess" again in that husky tone of his. I shouldn't yearn for his rough hands on my skin, and I hate myself for wanting a man who clearly doesn't want me for more than just my body.

After about five minutes of eating with all this tension, I can't handle being at the table anymore. My three men seem to be envisioning slowly killing the other three who joined our little fiesta, and the new three are bouncing between murderous stares, smug looks, and attempting to get Carmen's attention.

I'm trying to ignore the reality that I saw all of these men in a basement, torturing and killing. Secretly, I'm hoping those two deserved it, but that doesn't stop me from remembering the *pop* of the gun when they were shot in the head.

I've heard that sound before, and it still haunts me.

Quietly, and on shaking legs, I stand from my chair and motion to leave, but I'm stopped with a large hand on my arm.

Looking to the giant with an attitude, I snap, "I just need to go to the restroom."

"I'll come with you," he insists.

Absolutely fucking not.

My face flames as I realize that all eyes are on us. Zane watches me closely, like he's ready to grab my other arm, while Rio just smirks at our interaction. The attention from the men across the table is too keen for my liking and I attempt to swallow the lump forming in my throat.

Carmen interjects, "She's a grown woman, Ash. You don't need to watch her pee."

"Wouldn't be the first time," he mumbles, and I shoot a withering glare in his direction.

Before he can argue further, Carmen stands with me. "I'll show her. You can chill."

Glancing down at the brute still grasping my arm, I dart my eyes to the side, reminding him that we have an audience. But, of course, he and the rest of my damn wardens don't give a fuck.

A throat clears at the head of the table, and Asher reluctantly releases my arm once he makes eye contact with Paloma.

Taking the escape, she and Carmen are giving me, I scurry away. Carmen links her arm with mine as we walk away together and she lets out a sigh, making me think she needs to get away from the table just as badly as I do.

"I'm Carmen, by the way," she says with a kind smile as we step through the back door.

"Spencer."

"Yeah, I figured. Rio doesn't shut up about you."

My face heats at her comment and all words leave me.

"I'm sorry to bring all the drama here. It's not usually like that." She tilts her head to the side. "Okay, that's a lie—sometimes it is. But when you have five menstruating women all in one room, shit is bound to happen."

We round a corner that leads down a hallway covered in family pictures and it's hard to resist the urge to stop and find baby pictures of Rio.

"Don't worry about it. I'm an only child, so it's fun to see the family dynamics."

Carmen turns to me and widens her eyes. "I want to be clear, I didn't invite those guys here. Gabriel grew up with Rio, so he randomly shows up, and over the years he added Mateo and Diego."

Rio grew up with that violent psycho?

Regardless, my heart goes out to her—I understand.

Sometimes it's nice to have the attention of three attractive men.

But then you find out they kill people in their basement.

"I know what you mean. Sometimes you want to push them away, but they literally won't leave you alone."

Or they handcuff you to the fucking bed and then expect you to wear other women's clothes.

"It's complicated," Carmen says on a sigh while her shoulders fall forward as we stop before the bathroom door.

"I'm good with complicated," I emphasize with a head tilt. "I wish there was something I could do to help. God knows I'm not happy with Rio, Asher, and Zane right now either." *Most days, actually.*

"Well . . ." She trails off in thought, then gives me a mischievous smile. "Maybe there is."

CHAPTER 6

SPENCER

Carmen and I settle back at the table and give each other a quick glance. In the bathroom, she gave me a rundown of who's who, and a little bit about each. And I tried to explain how I was afraid of them, without giving any details. Carmen swore to me Gabriel, Diego, and Mateo would never hurt me simply because I'm family now.

Family . . . It's a strange concept—one I always longed for but couldn't have. Mom said she didn't need any more children when she had me, and I have my friends at Clay Creations and Abstract Dreams, but for someone to call me "family" feels different.

Paloma sits at the head of the table making idle chit chat with Gabriel who is seated to her left with Mateo, Carmen, Diego, and Mariela seated after him.

On Paloma's right is Solana followed by Zane, Asher, me, and Rio. Elena sits at the end of the table, quietly bickering with her younger sister, Mariela, about being present for family dinner.

My eyes meet Carmen's again, and she gives a subtle head tilt indicating the man on her right.

I clear my throat after I take a bite of food. "So, Mateo, is it?"

Mateo perks up as his eyes dart to the men on either side of me and a wicked smile appears on his face. "That's me, darling. And who are you?"

"None of your fucking business, Alvarez," Zane spits out at him.

I hope I'm not making a mistake . . . here goes nothing.

Ignoring Zane's warning, I reach across the table and shake Mateo's hand. "Spencer Gray. I'm an artist in Chelsea." I give him a flirty smile to add fuel to the fire.

Recognition dawns on his face. "Ah. So, you're the infamous girlfriend."

My heart skips a beat.

Is there anyone they haven't told?

Well, Zane and Rio did declare themselves my boyfriends at the hospital, but we've never discussed it. I naïvely thought the topic would float away, but clearly it hasn't.

Internally, I shake off my overthinking and go back to my attempt at flirting.

"It seems I'm at a disadvantage, Mateo. You know me, but I don't know much about you." I twirl a lock of hair around my finger.

That's what flirty girls do, right?

Yeah, in 80s movies.

"Spencer," Zane growls in warning. Asher keeps a passive look on his face but grabs his Corona in a death grip. Rio ignores his food and silently observes the scene in front of him with his hands balled into fists.

"My profession isn't nearly as creative as yours. I'm in to . . ."

He picks up his beer, swirls it like he's mixing expensive wine, and takes a sip. "Let's call it sales, customer service, and real estate." He gives me a wink and leans back in his chair. His eyes subtly wander to Carmen, but she ignores him as she takes small bites of her food.

Diego watches everything with keen intuition that reminds me of Zane.

"You mean you're a weapons and drug dealer who has a slew of prostitutes working for him, and you have the occasional turf war." Zane scoffs.

Mateo shrugs a shoulder. "Technically that last part falls under Diego's purview."

I ignore both of their comments and pretend that everything they just said doesn't make me shiver. I'm doing my girl Carmen a solid while at the same time getting payback of my own.

"Seems like you're a busy man with little time to play. Must be lonely."

Mateo leans towards me with his elbows on the table. "Maybe you can make it less lonely, darling."

There's a crash to my left, and I jump in my seat.

"The fuck she will!" Zane shoves his chair back, and it topples over. Rio's family stares at Zane like they've never seen this side of him. Mateo and Gabriel smirk while Diego keeps on observing.

Zane makes his way to me and hauls me out of my chair.

"What the hell are you doing?" I shoot at Zane as he grabs me by my hand and drags me across the yard. Everyone stares in disbelief, and my stomach drops.

Zane storms into the house with Rio hot on our heels. "We need to have a little talk."

"Like hell we do!" I shout. He takes me the same way Carmen did, and as we enter the bathroom, Rio shuts the door behind us. The bathroom isn't small, but it's not huge. With the three of us in here, the space is cramped.

I lean against the sink and glower at the two of them. "Okay, we're here. What now?"

"What the fuck was all that about?" Zane questions.

I cross my arms. "I don't know what you're talking about."

"*Esas son mentiras,*" Rio chimes in. *That's a lie.*

Zane points in the direction of the backyard. "Flirting with Mateo as if we're not sitting right there. Seriously?"

I shrug a shoulder like it's no big deal which only angers Zane more.

"What was the point? Explain it to us, Spence," Zane pleads.

My lips pinch together.

Zane narrows his gaze. "Make no mistake, Angel, you're ours. If you want the male population to stay at its current number, you will not flirt with every man that crosses your path."

"You don't get to tell me what to do, Zane Kingston!"

"He's right, Mama. No flirting."

My hands dig into the flesh at my arms. "You're. Not. The. Boss. Of. Me." I emphasize each word. "And where do you get off telling everyone I'm your girlfriend? We've never talked about it. You can't just claim me like that."

"We can and we did." Rio steps up to my side and pushes my hair over my shoulder, exposing my neck to him. He brings his mouth to my ear and whispers, "You know you love it, Mama."

How dare they!

Unable to hold back the question dancing on my tongue, I blurt out, "Whose clothes are in your closet?"

"What?" Zane and Rio ask together, befuddled.

"The damn woman's clothes in Zane's closet. Whose are

they? Do you really expect me to wear clothing from your past hookups? And let's not forget y'all fucking kidnapped me!" Anger, mixed with hurt, drips from my tone.

"The clothes are yours," Zane answers plainly.

My brows pinch together. "Huh?"

Rio's voice grows soft. "We bought them for you, Spencer. We knew you'd end up at our house eventually and wanted you to feel welcome."

"You bought them for . . ." My voice trails off.

"You, Angel. They're yours."

"But how—"

Zane exchanges a knowing look with Rio and says, "I've had my hands on your body multiple times. You think I wouldn't be able to guess your size?"

Rio beams at me. "As for the supposed 'kidnapping,' let's call it what it really is: a sleepover. We're testing out what it's like to live together, and I think it's going good so far. Yeah, there's been some handcuffs involved, but those will go away soon, and we'll be one big happy family."

Zane and Rio take advantage while I stand there stunned in silence.

They sandwich me between them, and goosebumps spread over my skin. I try to keep my mind clear, but then Rio kisses his way down my neck. I gasp, and Zane trails his finger down my left arm.

"Give in, Angel." Zane hooks his finger under my chin and turns my head his direction. "Be angry all you want, but at the end of the day you belong to us."

Zane seals his lips to mine in a demanding kiss. I open my mouth to him when his tongue swipes at the seam of my lips. Zane lets out a deep groan when his tongue gets a taste of me. He dominates my mouth while his hand wraps around my throat.

Zane pulls away and turns to Rio, giving my neck a small squeeze. "How wet is she?"

Rio smiles as his tattooed hand unbuttons my pants and disappears in my panties. His eyes light up when he discovers what I already know.

I'm drenched, and it's just from their simple touches, gentle words, and a kiss.

I squirm as Rio drags his fingers back and forth along my slit. When his hands leave my panties, he holds his fingers up to show Zane.

Zane leans forward, takes Rio's fingers into his mouth and sucks.

Rio groans. "That was mine to taste."

Zane's tone turns assertive. "You can lick her next time. Right now, she's going to come on my fingers." Then they work together, on either side of me, pulling my jeans and panties down to my ankles.

I'm panting, and they've barely touched me. I'm like an animal in heat, but only they have the ability to satisfy me.

I clench my thighs together and look to both of them with pleading eyes.

"What do you need, Angel?"

"You," I answer. "Both of you." With confidence I don't feel, I grab them by their shirts and pull them closer.

Zane teases my hip with his fingertip while Rio inches my shirt up, revealing my black, lace bra.

"You can do better than that, Spencer," Rio says as his mouth grazes over the top of my breasts. "Tell us exactly what you need." He lightly drags his teeth over the lace covering my nipple.

My cheeks get hot. I've never been good at dirty talk, but I'm desperate for them. There's an intense fluttering in my stomach.

I need them and I need them now.

My hands leave their shirts, and I pull their faces close to mine. "Make me come." Then, before I chicken out, I slam my mouth on Rio's and pour my passion and all my desire into the kiss.

"Always, Angel."

Zane's fingers stop teasing and dive right for my pussy. Rio pushes me to sit on the counter; and together, he and Zane spread my knees, exposing my center to them. I try to snap my legs closed, but they each have a firm grip and refuse to let go.

"You can't hide anymore, Spencer. You can't hide how much you want us—how much you need us. Your desire is dripping from your perfect pussy."

Zane's dirty words make me moan into Rio's mouth. I moan louder when Zane plunges a finger into my needy core. As he pumps that finger in and out, over and over, wet sounds echo through the bathroom, proving how much they turn me on.

Rio's other hand trails up my inner thigh and his fingers rub circles around my clit. When I rock my hips, Zane adds another finger, making me cry out.

Rio pulls his mouth from mine, and says in a husky voice, "You're so wet for us, Mama. So desperate. How badly do you want to come?"

When I don't answer, he pulls my bra down. My nipples are already stiff and become as hard as diamonds as he admires my body.

Rio covers one nipple with his mouth and sucks hard. I whimper as the sensation shoots straight to my clit. They're making it hard to think, let alone form sentences.

Rio's mouth let's go with a *pop*. "Tell us. How badly do you want it?"

When I still don't answer, he bites down on my breast,

causing me to cry out. Zane covers my mouth with his, muffling out my sounds. The sting from the bite intensifies the pleasure from their hands. I rock my hips faster, searching for my release.

Zane leans back at the same time Rio lets go. I look down and there's red teeth marks right above my nipple where Rio bit me.

"So bad. I fucking need it. Please. Please make me come," I beg.

Zane's fingers inside me begin rubbing that sensitive spot while Rio's fingers strum my clit rapidly. I detonate as my pussy spasms. Waves of pleasure roll over me and I swear I black out.

When I come to, Zane and Rio's hands still haven't left my core. Instead, they're gently stroking me as my orgasm fades. Zane is kissing me like a man starved, and Rio is sucking on my neck.

I expect them to pull away and leave me to clean myself up. Zane took care of me yesterday, but is that really the norm? Asher also did it, but I can't think about that now with how complicated everything is with him.

Once my heart calms and I'm breathing normally again, Zane removes his hand and licks his dripping fingers clean. Then he grabs Rio's face and slams his lips on Rio's. They move together in a passionate kiss with dueling tongues. The passion and adoration between them fills my heart.

My inner muscles clench around nothing but air as I watch them. I didn't know they were together, or maybe it's the heat of the moment. I shouldn't stare, but it's okay because they're literally right in front of me, right?

"You taste like perfection, Mama."

Before I can stop myself, I babble. "Are you two together? Like *together* together? And that would make us, what? A throuple? Because . . . We just . . . And . . . Is this temporary? Us.

Are we temporary? Y'all realize we have a lot to talk about, right? We should probably discuss the basement, the guns and knives that you always carry, how all of this will work—"

Zane covers my mouth with his hand. "Babe, slow down. Yes, Rio and I are together. We have an open relationship."

Pushing out an angry breath, I glare.

"Yes, Angel. I know you're the jealous type. We won't sleep with anyone else."

"I don't need anyone else when I have you two," Rio adds.

"As for how this will work, I'm not sure. We'll take it one day at a time. We can discuss the rest at home, okay?"

Nodding my head, he removes his hand.

Home.

Blushing furiously, I look away retreating into myself as a I brace for the loneliness to come next, but neither of them let go of my legs as Zane grabs a cloth from the shelf above the toilet and wets it in the sink behind me. He cleans up the mess I made then gives me a tender kiss.

Tears form in my eyes, and I do my best to hold them back, but they spring free when Rio takes a turn kissing me. These kisses are different from the ones a few seconds ago—they're soft and sweet, filled with devotion.

Zane wipes my tears as Rio puts my pants back on.

"You're our everything. Don't forget that, Angel."

Once Rio buttons my jeans, I look down in confusion— something feels weird. Then I see Rio hold up my black thong. I grab for it, but he raises his hand, yanking them out of my reach.

"These are mine," he says with a smirk then brings them to his nose and inhales before he stuffs them into his pocket and leads the way back outside.

Before we reach the back door, Zane's phone buzzes. He

peers at it and mumbles something about "stupid cops" and Asher being on stakeout duty.

I keep my face composed as I take my seat at the table, but I turn a deep shade of red when I feel Asher's gaze zero in on my neck.

Shit. Did Rio leave a hickey?

I cover it up with my hair and dig back into my food, hoping that if I don't talk about it, we can pretend no one knew what happened in the bathroom.

Mateo not so quietly whispers to Carmen, "Maybe you, Diego, Gabriel, and I need to take a trip to the bathroom too."

Carmen chokes on her food, and I cover my face, absolutely mortified.

CHAPTER 7

SPENCER

After dinner, the men involved in the scuffle are forced to clear the table and wash all the dishes by hand. Throughout the cleanup, each side takes little jabs at each other. They whisper insults, trip each other, and exchange scowls.

These scary men, each with a body count that's likely higher than I can count, have reduced themselves to squabbling children.

While they clean, Paloma leads me to the couch with a mug of Mexican hot cocoa. I could take this as an opportunity to rat out the guys, but I find myself incapable of forming the words. Instead, I want to soak in the love Paloma gifts so freely. I didn't realize how starved I was for a mother's gentle touch.

Across the room, Solana sits in a chair by the window, overlooking the backyard, still reading. Elena left right after we finished eating when she got a call to go into work—she's a trauma surgeon at St. Barnabas Hospital. Mariela left claiming she had a date, and Carmen tried to dip as well but none of the five angry men were having it. She's currently at the kitchen table chewing on her nails and ignoring the pointed looks she keeps getting while studying for the LSATs.

Asher is keeping her company at the table since he wasn't involved in the skirmish.

I'm settling in when Paloma joins me with her own mug; I almost spit my warm chocolatey drink all over the living room when Paloma asks, "So tell me, which of my boys are you with?" I choke and cough like I'm about to hack up a lung. "Or is it all three?"

My chin dips down as I look anywhere but her, and I stammer, "I—Umm—Well—"

Paloma sets our mugs on the coffee table, gently grabs my hand, and pats the top of it. "It's all right. No need to be alarmed. There's no judgement here, *mija*."

When I finally pick my head up and look into her eyes, I know she means it. She isn't that crazy mom who chases away her son's girlfriend. She doesn't criticize what she doesn't know. She doesn't condemn what isn't considered normal.

"It's a bit complicated at the moment," I finally get out.

She nods her head. "Isn't it always. What's love without a little complexity?"

My puzzling look spurs her to continue. "Let me give you some advice, Spencer. Zane would rip his heart out and give it to you—remember what a precious gift that is. Even couples who have been married for decades can't say that about their partner."

Is that what's actually happening right now?

"Rio is protective and it's an instinct he can't turn off. Let him, and he will do whatever it takes to keep you safe and grant you vengeance." She says the statement with a surety that tells me she's familiar with that side of him.

This is getting weird . . . Vengeance?

"And lastly, Asher. That boy has seen too much—they all

have. But it affects him differently. He may seem hard and cold, but he's not. Give him time."

But he is hard and cold!

Is he though?

Damn, Intrusive Spencer. I don't want to think about the *incident* in my kitchen and how he was soft with me after and carefully put me to bed. Because the other side of him, that I see way more often than not, is a brick wall.

All I can do is nod along as Paloma makes it harder and harder to be angry with my men.

Turning towards the kitchen, I find Zane and Rio flicking water at the gangbangers who seem to be obsessed with Carmen. All five of them are giggling like little boys, causing a smile to form on my face and satisfaction to swell in my chest. As if he can sense the shift in mood, Asher's eyes meet mine while he sits at the kitchen table. The corner of his mouth tugs up and my smile falters. I look down at my hands as they wring together in my lap, and I consider Paloma's words.

Yes, I've been held against my will, but . . . maybe I'm okay with it. There hasn't been a moment where I actually thought they'd hurt me, or do something I don't want them to.

I don't want to give in so easily, though. I don't want them to think everything is okay.

Orgasms don't equate to forgiveness.

"Tell me about your family. Rio said you're not from New York."

My mouth flaps open and closed as I think about how to answer a question I've avoided for years. "Oh. Um. No, I didn't grow up here. I'm from Texas."

"Ooo. A southern belle. I like that," she comments with a warm pat on my arm. "I'm sure your mother misses you."

"Uh. Yes, she does."

Shit. Mom.

She must be worried about me. The distance has been hitting her harder, and now I don't have my damn phone so I can reassure her that I'm fine. I'm going to need to talk to the guys about getting my phone back—I highly doubt they'll go for it, but might as well try.

Paloma either sees the far off look in my eyes or she's oblivious to my quandary. She rises from the couch, gathering our now-empty mugs, and says, just like any good mother would, "Let me go find some baby photos of Rio. I have some cute ones from when he said he wanted to be Spiderman when he grew up."

Aww! Little Spiderman Rio.

While I fidget in my seat, unsure of what I'm supposed to do in this situation, Solana meanders over and sits next to me. Her book is closed, and her eyes dart between me and the kitchen.

"Zane told me you asked him to read *New Moon*. How are you liking the series?"

She gives a small smile. "I didn't ask him to, he volunteered. He's kind like that."

Her admiration gives the impression of a sisterly love. A love that's made of holidays spent together and laughs shared over many family dinners.

I glance over into the kitchen and see that they're finishing up putting away the large feast.

"Go easy on him," she whispers gently.

My attention snaps back to Solana. "What?"

"Rio—all of them really—but Rio is a good brother. Overprotective at times, yes. But he's never mean; he just worries."

Feeling another lecture coming on, I just nod along, but Solana drops a bomb instead.

"It wasn't easy growing up in this house after everything with Izzy; I know I've been sheltered a bit more. Mariela acts out and Carmen loses herself in studies, but I'm the baby, so it's like having five parents instead of just one." She shrugs a shoulder, accepting her lot in life.

But my mind hangs on another detail . . .

"Who's Izzy?"

Solana plays with a stray thread on her jeans. "Our sister."

Dipping my head to get closer, I lower my voice. "What happened to her?"

Solana finally returns her eyes to me and answers, "She died."

CHAPTER 8

RIO

*A*fter we left my childhood home, I was able to breathe a bit easier. Gabriel wouldn't dare lay a finger on Spencer, not after I've made it clear that she's ours—not just mine and Zane's. She's Asher's too, even if he won't admit it yet.

Once we got back to our brownstone, Spencer wouldn't make eye contact with me and went straight to Zane's room. The lock clicked into place after she shut the door.

We decided to forego the handcuffs since she seemed to finally be on board with being ours after our bathroom activity.

She looked like she was processing everything that was said, and I should give her space to do so. But that was over twelve hours ago. Zane and Asher both left for work, and locks were meant to be picked . . . right?

If Zane would just give me a key to his room, I wouldn't have to do this song and dance.

Setting aside my lock pick set, I open the door and make my way into the room on quiet feet. I find Spencer peering into the closet and scanning through her new wardrobe, getting ready for the day. My eyes go straight to her ass that's in a new pair of panties, seeing as I took the thong she was wearing yesterday. Lace traces the curves of her cheeks, and I feel myself grow hard.

As my gaze wanders upward, I'm met with silky smooth skin.

No shirt. No bra.

Is this heaven?

When Spencer finally feels my eyes on her, she turns and lets out a yelp, jumping backward into the closet and covering her beautiful tits with her arm.

"How the hell did you get in here?"

Widening my eyes, I point to the door.

"I swear I locked it . . ." Her voice trails off.

My only answer is to shrug my shoulders and drink in all of her skin on display for my viewing pleasure. The way her waist flares out to her perfect hips, the way her breasts are pressed against her arm.

What I wouldn't give to have them in my face again like they were yesterday.

I should feel ashamed for doing what we did in the bathroom of my childhood home, but remorse is not a feeling I'm familiar with. When you do and say what you mean, you have no regrets.

Spencer's cheeks turn a beautiful shade of pink as she notices the bulge in my jeans. Her lips flatten. "You could look away."

Raising a brow, I cross my arms and lean back. With a smirk, I reply, "So could you," and gesture to my dick.

"I'm the one that's barely dressed!"

I came in here to check on her and get her to talk to me, but those plans flew out the window when I got a look at that delectable ass.

"I could get undressed if you want." Prowling towards her, I continue. "I could drop to my knees right here and drag those panties down your sexy legs with my teeth, then worship you the way I've dreamed of for weeks."

Her breaths become short and more frequent, causing her tits to stick out more around her arm in a way that would make any man weak in the knees.

I want to see my cum smeared across her luscious mounds.

Marking her, claiming her.

With my height, I tower over her frame. I lean down so my mouth is at her ear, but we don't touch anywhere else. Taking her lobe between my teeth, I give it a little tug, and she lets out a moan.

"Is that what you want, Mama? Do you want me on my knees, tonguing that wet cunt?"

With her free hand, she pushes on my chest, and I respect her decision by taking a step backward. But only a small step.

Like, an inch.

"You should not be in here while I'm like this."

"Like what? Naked?"

"Yes! I'm naked, and you're fully clothed. The power imbalance here is strong. Not that I think you should get naked with me right now—or ever. I don't expect that. There are zero expectations in that department."

I bite my lip to keep the smile at bay. "You should have very high expectations when it comes to us getting naked together, Mama."

Lust and need fill her eyes, but there's a hint of hesitation. Not the kind that only needs a little encouragement to disappear. This hesitation hints at a dilemma.

"What is it, Spencer?"

She nibbles at her lip. "Maybe we can talk about this when I'm clothed?"

"No need to get dressed on my account. I'm not offended by your body in the slightest." I drag my gaze up and down her curvy body to emphasize my point.

"That's—uhhh—nice." She cringes. "Could you turn around?"

"Nope."

"No?" Spencer blinks rapidly.

I shake my head in answer.

Her nostrils flare as she lets out a frustrated breath. "Fine." She reaches behind her and grabs the first few things her hand lands on—a band tee and leggings—then she stomps off to the bathroom to change, and I keep my eyes glued to that jiggling ass as she walks away.

WHEN SPENCER RETURNS from the bathroom, I'm lying on the bed with my hands resting behind my head and my ankles crossed. She walks in timidly, and I quickly realize it's because she still doesn't have a bra on.

Thank God.

I'm all about freeing the tits.

She stands at the end of Zane's bed, fidgeting with her hands.

"No need to be shy, Spencer. Come here. Make yourself comfortable."

The shy look in her eye turns to skepticism as she makes her way to the opposite side and sits cross-legged, facing me. Before she can react, I snag her around the waist and lay her on top of me. My arms circle her waist, preventing her from pulling away.

"Rio!"

"Much better." I give her a self-satisfied smile.

She narrows her eyes, and her face has a pinched expression.

"Tell me what's on your mind, Mama."

Her eyes wander to the side. "I don't know what you're talking about."

"No more secrets, Spencer. Talk to me."

Spencer concentrates on the collar of my shirt as she ponders her next words, running her hands up and down my chest.

If she does that much longer, I'm going to fuck her right here on this bed.

That's not a bad idea.

Clearing her throat she says, "Solana and I talked a little bit."

My body tenses. I'm not sure what Spencer and my baby sister discussed, but by Spencer's demeanor, I can assume it's not how I wore Spiderman boxers through my teens.

I've never cared too much about what people think. It's not in my nature, but for some reason, I care. I care what Spencer will think when she knows the truth.

CHAPTER 9

SPENCER

Rio's muscles go taut under my hands, and when I look up, Rio's focus is elsewhere. I bring my hand to his face and smooth the tension between his brows with my fingers. He's never serious like that around me, and I don't want that to start now.

This may be a serious conversation, but I don't want to drag him down. I need him to be the Rio I know and love.

No. Not love. Nope.

Not yet.

Fucking hell.

"She told me about——"

"Izzy." His voice is tight.

"Yeah." The struggle I see in him sits heavy on my chest. "You don't need to tell me about her—you don't owe me answers. I just wanted to say that I'm sorry. I'm sorry you lost her."

His face turns to the side, so I gently place my hands on his cheeks and bring his attention back to me. When his eyes connect with mine, I reassure him. "I'm here. You've made sure I'm not going anywhere." I chuckle.

Therapists everywhere are shaking their heads at me. Using humor to cope in a situation like this probably isn't healthy—I learned that much from the few books I've read.

"I want to tell you. I said no more secrets, and I meant that." The seriousness of his tone shuts me up, but I continue to comfort him by smoothing my hand over his short hair and drawing circles on his scalp.

He inhales deeply, letting out a long breath, then gets a far off look in his eyes. "I was ten years old when Isabella went missing. Elena was six, and Carmen wasn't born yet. We were playing with her in the front yard while my mom was putting the groceries away. We were kicking a soccer ball back and forth. Izzy was just three and wanted to prove she could play just as hard and fast as Elena and I. She kicked the ball extra hard, and the ball went flying into the bushes. Elena and I both went after it. The bushes used to be thicker and were difficult to dig into—our backs were only turned for a couple minutes. When we turned around, she was gone."

My heart sinks as I watch the anger and defeat take hold of him. "I'm so sorry."

Rio clears his throat and continues. "About a week later, Gabriel and I were walking home from putting up fliers in the neighborhood. I passed an alleyway but turned back when I noticed something small and pink sticking out from behind the dumpster." He swallows. "It was her shoes."

Gasping, I cover my mouth with my hand.

"Her clothes were dirty and disheveled, like someone hadn't put them back on right."

Horror takes over my features, and my voice is almost inaudible. "No."

"I didn't know I was screaming until a crowd had gathered.

Gabriel was trying to pull me off her which earned him two black eyes. I couldn't stop holding my baby sister—her skin was so cold."

Tears spill down my cheeks as Rio sits up and situates himself so he's sitting up with his back against the headboard. My knees fall to either side of his hips, and I wrap my arms around his neck, bringing my chest to his. Rio's breathing his labored, his heartbeat is erratic.

"I'm so sorry," I choke out on a sob, but I try to not invade this moment with my own feelings. I need to be strong for him. He deserves that much from me. "Did they catch the person who did it?"

Rio's lips curl. "You could say that."

My brows squish together, and I lean back so I can see his face.

"There was . . . DNA evidence, but the fucker wasn't in the system." He glares over my shoulder. "There was a man who lived down the street. Darryl Williams. He was leading the charge in our neighborhood to help find witnesses, evidence, things like that. He had also begun dating my mom a few weeks before. He'd come by with flowers and other things my mom liked."

My stomach hollows out and the breakfast sandwich Zane left outside the door is ready to make a reappearance.

"None of us noticed how he paid Izzy too much attention. He finally slipped up in front of the lead detective on the case when he mentioned the color of Izzy's socks. That wasn't public record, and my mom was catatonic during the whole thing, so we know she didn't tell Darryl that detail. The detective was able to get a warrant to swab Darryl's mouth. His DNA was a match. After he was arrested, they found a hidden door behind a book-shelf in his living room. It was full of child pornography."

I clutch Rio tighter while his hands begin to shake.

"He only served two years."

"What?!" I rear back in disbelief.

That asshole is still out there? How many children has he hurt since then?

"He was able to get a lawyer who wanted to make a name for himself. The guy was able to appeal the conviction and get the DNA evidence thrown out."

"Oh my God."

The horror this man has endured. This happy, charming, fun man.

My happy, charming, fun man.

"But then I caught up to him. That *cabrón* kept his house while he was in prison and thought he could move back in without any repercussions." Rio looks me right in the eye as he says, "One night, while he slept, I snuck in and handed out the justice Izzy deserved. Gabriel followed me and helped me tie that asshole to a kitchen chair and I bloodied my fists with his filth."

Tears spill down my cheeks as Rio's pain, coated in anger, rolls off him and fills the room.

"Getting raped in prison was supposed to be enough? That's not nearly enough! He took my sister! My Izzy!" He pounds his chest, emphasizing the last two words. "My mom didn't get out of bed for months. Elena didn't speak for a year. And two years in prison was all he got? Fuck that."

My bottom lip wobbles as I listen to him.

"I can't unsee what I've seen, Spencer. Uncles corrupting nieces, mothers selling children, neighbors kidnapping infants down the street. It never ends. There are too many, and there's not enough on our side to fight them all. But that doesn't mean I'll stop. I'll never stop. I'll tear every fucker limb from limb, because this devil doesn't just thirst for their blood. He bathes in it."

Sheepishly, I ask, "So, you only kill bad people?"

"Yeah, Mama. Only bad people."

Understanding spreads through me.

I've always believed that knowledge is power. But what people forget is that knowledge also comes with responsibility.

What would I have done? If the man who had killed my baby sister got off because a lawyer was able to convince some idiots that the police were wrong, what would I do? If I had witnessed what Rio has, how would that change me? Could I kill the people responsible too?

I'm not sure I can answer these questions.

Murder is wrong, but isn't that what the government is allowed to do? They can hand out the death penalty like free candy to convicts if they wish. What's supposed to happen when the justice system fails? What happens when a killer goes free?

While I battle back and forth in my mind, Rio watches me silently. I don't like that he's quiet—that's not the man I know. He always knows how to lighten the mood.

I guess I'll just have to do that for him.

CHAPTER 10

SPENCER

*R*io waits unsuspectingly while I gather my courage. I've never initiated intimacy with a man before, but with Rio, I want to.

He watches me carefully. "Did I scare you?"

"No. I'm not afraid."

Let's hope I know what I'm doing.

Sitting up, I slide my hand down his chest. I cherish each muscle I feel beneath the fabric of his shirt. I pause when I reach the top of his pants, and my brow raises in question. "Do you want me?"

"Is that a real question?"

The steel in his jeans grows hard as my hand waits just above it.

"Answer me, Rio. Do you want me?"

"More than my next breath, Mama."

Here goes nothing.

Gripping the hem of my shirt, I raise my hands and toss the material aside. The cool air makes me shiver as it kisses my bare skin. When it graces over my breasts, my nipples turn hard. My body aches for him and the pleasure I know he can pull from me.

"Then have me, Rio." I don't recognize my own voice. I sound like a confident, sexy siren.

"Shit. You don't have to tell me twice."

I squeal when Rio moves faster than I thought possible and flips us. My legs part as Rio settles between them.

"Once I have this pussy, it's mine, Spencer—there's no going back. So you better be sure, right here, right now. I'm not going to change who I am to make you feel comfortable. I'm not a bad man, but I'm not a good one either. So be sure. Tell me 'yes' again with that beautiful voice."

In this moment, I know that, in my heart, we can make this work. I may not like his methods, but he does good in the world, whether he sees it or not.

"Yes, Rio. Make me yours."

Rio groans. "Fucking finally."

In the blink of an eye, my pants are gone and all that's left is the lacy pair of panties Rio found me in earlier. His eyes wander my body, intensifying the ache building in my core.

"Please, Rio."

"You never need to beg with me, Spencer. *Puedes pedir lo que quieras, y yo te lo daría.*" *You can ask me for anything, and I will give it to you.*

Rio grips my leg and begins kissing his way up my body, utilizing his tongue and teeth to rachet my need higher and higher. When he gets to my hip, he uses his teeth to drag my panties down my legs, and I lift my hips to help.

Once I'm bare to him, he stares at the apex of my thighs like it's the best present he's ever received. My arousal glistens as it slides down my inner thighs.

Rio's nostrils flare. The muscles throughout his body are

strained like he's holding himself back. "Just one taste, Baby Girl. That's all I need."

My only response is to bend my knees and let them fall to either side.

Rio groans, "Fuck me," then he dives right in. He licks me from my puckered hole to my sensitive hood and circles around it.

Rio looks up; there's a fire in his eyes, burning white hot. "I lied. One taste is never going to be enough." Then he leans back down and sucks my clit into his mouth.

Whimpering, I raise my hips to meet each lash of his tongue against my delicate flesh. Before long, I'm a moaning puddle of pleasure and there's a pressure building deep inside me, ready to send me over the edge.

While Rio's tongue flicks my bud back and forth, he works two fingers into my pussy and does a scissoring motion inside me. His rough fingers pet my G spot, and his tongue picks up speed.

My pussy contracts as I reach the peak, oblivion clouds my vision, and I cry out, screaming his name. The pulsing of my pussy around Rio's digits continues, and I ride my orgasm for as long as possible.

As I come back down to earth, Rio gets up on his knees, reaching for the top of his pants. I pop up and smack his hands out of the way.

"Let me," I say as I look up at him through my lashes.

"Anything you want, Baby."

Once I have his pants undone, and his erect cock springs free, I peel them down his tattooed thighs. I get a glimpse of various pictures and symbols across his legs. Flowers, a calavera, and fire are some of the images I'm able to make out.

He helps me get his pants off, then swiftly removes his shirt by reaching behind him and pulling the material over his head in one swoop. The tattoos that are revealed put me in a trance.

I lean back on my elbows and admire his gorgeous, bronze, inked skin, his length so hard it almost looks painful. I want to run my tongue over every inch, but before I can lean in for a lick, I yelp as Rio grabs me by the hips and flips me onto my stomach.

"Rio?"

"Cheek to the mattress and ass in the air, Baby Girl."

I get into position right away, and groan into the sheets when I feel his hot breath brush against my center. His tongue is on my pussy again, but then he travels up to that tight hole—somewhere no one has ever touched. Rio circles it with his tongue over and over.

"Tell me, Spencer. Has anyone ever taken you here?"

I shake my head in reply.

Then I feel the blunt tip of his cock at my core. He slowly pushes in while simultaneously breaching that ring of muscle with his finger. My whole frame tightens.

"Relax for me. Let me in."

After a few deep breaths, his finger and cock are all the way inside me.

"This is what it could be like, Baby Girl. When Zane and I take you together for the first time, we can do it just like this—one of us in your needy pussy and one of us in this virgin ass."

My pussy flutters around his shaft as the picture his words paint forms in my mind.

"Oh yeah. You want that, Baby."

Fucking hell, this man's dirty talk.

We moan together as Rio holds onto my hip with one hand, pulls out of my warm wet center, and thrusts back in. His finger follows the motion as well. The sensation it causes is not one I'm prepared for.

"Dammit, Spencer. You feel so good. So good, gripping my cock like that."

He goes in and out again. And again. His hips pick up speed as he retreats and slams back into me over and over.

"Shit, Spencer. Come with me. I can't hold off much longer."

Without waiting for a response, he reaches around and zeroes in on my clit. He pinches it, and I erupt, drowning in overwhelming pleasure, as Rio follows me right into the abyss.

Once my body relaxes again, I feel Rio plastered to my back.

"Fuck, Spencer. My legs almost gave out on me. *¿Intentas matarme?*" *Are you trying to kill me?* "Death by pussy."

I snort, and a full belly laugh overtakes me as Rio rolls to his side and joins me in laughing at his antics.

As our snickering ends, our eyes lock, and this moment of pure happiness burrows itself into my heart. The way he looks at me . . . it's like I'm the most treasured person in his world. To be that cared for by someone is a gift. One that I can't throw away.

Rio kisses my cheek then stalks to the bathroom, a renewed pep in his step.

I don't know why I'm surprised when he comes back with a wet cloth and cleans me up. This kind of treatment is going to take some getting used to.

But multiply this by three?

I think I just might sign on the dotted line.

CHAPTER 11

ZANE

ubbing my eyes, I give myself a small reprieve from staring at this damn case file. Liam and I have interviewed everyone possible, and there's still no sign of Ava Thomas.

Hank hasn't even heard anything. I'm close to resorting to searching every damn warehouse, abandoned building, and crack house in New York. Cain has to be using one of them as his new prep house after Asher, Rio, and I raided the last one. We found it after we busted the so-called "party" Cain had put on.

"Is there another informant? Someone besides Hank?"

I sigh. "Not unless you've turned anyone recently."

Liam looks just as ragged as I do. His baby is having a hard time sleeping at night, and it's showing in his appearance today. Poor guy is on his fourth cup of coffee, and it's not even lunchtime yet.

I'm not much better off. I stopped counting how many cups I've had after I got to three. One would think that finally sleeping with the woman of my dreams would settle me. But I feel like I'm losing my goddamn mind. This morning I couldn't find my badge—I practically tore Rio's room apart, searching for it. I even tiptoed into my bedroom while Spencer slept and dug around in there. After giving up on the search, I got to work, opened the top drawer of my desk, and found it sitting there, right on top.

"Let's start at the beginning and go back over everything, start to finish. That's what you always say to do when we're stuck, right?"

Rubbing my eyes, I answer, "Right."

Liam stands and begins to pace. "Ava was kidnapped outside Sunny's Market. Her sister, Ella, saw Ava get taken by two men who drove off in a white van. From Ella's description, we assume that Ava was subdued with chloroform. Then we have five other missing persons reports of women from ages twelve to twenty-five, and that's just the ones on our case load." He pauses in his path and rubs the back of his neck, staring at the floor. "What if they're all connected? Am I crazy for thinking that?"

Smart man.

"Do you have any evidence suggesting they're connected?"

Liam's hands rest on his hips and heaves a sigh. "Just my gut."

My head nods. "Then keep digging."

"What?" Liam's head snaps up.

"Trust your gut, but you need evidence to back it up."

Scratching his head, Liam paces again. The guy is going to wear a hole into the weathered tile if he does this much longer. "Okay, okay. Evidence. Right." He plops down in his chair and types away on his keyboard.

When Liam starts making calls, my phone vibrates on my desk. Picking it up, I check the GPS notification.

Goddammit, Dustin.

"I have to leave early today," I comment as I rise from my chair, gathering my things. "I'll see you tomorrow. Let me know if you come up with anything."

Liam nods with his phone to his ear as I pass his desk.

Traffic is awful, but it feels like it takes longer than normal. When I'm at a dead-stop, waiting for traffic to move, I shoot off a message to Asher, asking him to meet us at home.

Keeping my composure is difficult when I know I have two perfect people waiting at home for me, and my agitation grows as I realize I won't be able to spend time with Spencer and her luscious body.

Fucking Dustin. Again.

When I pull up to the brownstone, I jump out of my car and bound up the steps, taking them two at a time. Entering through the front door, I'm hit with the smell of sex.

The scent of Rio and Spencer's love-making makes my dick harden.

Why did I go to work again today?

My focus snaps to Rio, who is digging through the fridge. Shutting the door quietly, I sneak up on him from behind.

He's bent down, riffling through the produce, completely oblivious to my presence, when I wrap my arm around his neck and haul him into my chest. I secure my hold by grasping my wrist with my opposite hand. Rio struggles, accidentally kicking the refrigerator door closed, until he hears my voice.

With my lips right next to his ear, I whisper, "What have you been up to today?" Then I take his ear in my mouth and scrape my teeth over it.

"Fuuuuuuuuck," Rio groans.

Releasing my wrist, Rio falls forward an inch. I whip him around and push him up against the fridge door. "Tell me something, how did she feel?"

A roguish smile spreads across his face. "Like you don't already know."

Our bodies slam together at the same time and our mouths glue together in a passionate kiss. I get his bottom lip between my teeth and bite.

"I didn't take you for a jealous lover, Z."

"I'm not," I growl. "I hate that I wasn't here to participate. Speaking of, where is Spencer?"

Rio grips the front of my shirt, bringing us back together. He grinds his erection into me, and I hold back a moan. "I fucked her so hard and so good, on every surface in the house, and now she's worn out and asleep. We did it on the kitchen counter, in the shower, on the couch, in your bed . . ."

We're about to go back at each other when my phone buzzes again.

Shit.

Another notification about Dustin.

Fuck this guy. I hate that we need him.

I wish he would just die in a ditch.

I turn my phone around to show the screen to Rio. We break apart and begin discussing what to do about the prick. When Rio and I finish putting our plan together, Asher walks through the front door.

"Why the fuck does it smell like sex in here?" he asks with a wrinkled nose.

"Well, *pendejo*, when two people are attracted to each other—"

"I know how sex works, dumbass," Asher interrupts then plops himself on the couch. He stretches his arms above his head, causing a few pops to come from his body, then leans his head back against the top of the couch and closes his eyes. "Okay, I'm here. What's going on?"

Rio slaps Asher on the shoulder as we pass him on our way out. "You're on Spencer duty."

Asher sits up. "The fuck I am."

I show him my phone.

"Ah, shit. Fine. But I'm not reading her a bedtime story."

Rio snorts. *"Ya está dormida." She's already sleeping.*

"It's the afternoon. Why is she . . . never mind, I don't want to know."

After Rio walks out laughing, I turn to Asher. "Don't hurt her."

He turns stone cold. "There's nothing going on."

"Bullshit. Don't play stupid, Ash. I know something happened the other night at her apartment. That woman loves food, but she somehow fell asleep before we could get there with her dinner."

Ash winces. He may be composed, but we all know how to push each other's buttons. "It was a mistake. It won't happen again."

I shake my head at him. "You're an idiot."

"What?"

"I didn't stutter. It's obvious she cares about you. I saw the letter she left you. The trash isn't exactly a great hiding place." I let out a sigh, done with this argument. "She's not Rachel. Don't confuse the two. Rachel was selfish and then drowned in her grief—she didn't want our help. In the end, we weren't enough for her. Spencer isn't like that."

"Then why did she try to run?" he bites back.

I head for the door but turn back before I exit. "You know the answer. We all do."

THE BEGINNING of our drive is quiet. It's a long way to La Guardia, and Rio's smug attitude has faded as he stares out the window. He didn't even try to fight me on the music when I put on Green Day.

"Talk to me," I prompt him.

"If we want her to be truly ours, we have to tell her everything."

He's telling me what I already know. I may not be excited to relive the torment I endured, but for her, I'd endure it all over again.

"I told her about Izzy."

My head snaps around to him. The car swerves, earning me a few honks. "What?"

"I had to tell her. Solana told her a bit, so when Spencer asked, I told her the truth."

"Shit." I drag my hand through my hair. "What about Asher?"

"What about him?"

"You walked in on them kissing and we both know something happened with them the other night."

"What's between them is between them. After Rachel, I'm surprised Asher is willing to be with anyone at all. We can step in if he hurts her, but until then, we should let them figure it out on their own."

Just the thought of anyone hurting her has me grinding my teeth—even if it's my best friend. No one hurts my Angel.

Switching topics, I hand Rio my phone with the map open, showing him the dot we're following on the screen. "Looks like he's still heading for La Guardia," I inform Rio as I weave through traffic.

"How? He doesn't have fingers. *No dedos significa que no manejas.*" *No fingers means no driving.* Rio laughs as his own joke.

I can't help but to roll my eyes. "He's probably on the

subway or something." My focus darts back and forth between the blue dot on my phone and the crazy drivers on the road.

"*No me gusta que lo necesitemos, pero lo entiendo,*" Rio complains. *I don't like that we need him, but I get it.* "Ash's stakeout of Euphoria didn't give us shit. So now we need this *pendejo.*" *Asshole.*

When we arrive at the airport, I don't bother parking in a proper parking spot. I pull up to the curb and show the angry ramp agent my police badge. She shakes her head at me and grumbles a not-so-quiet *"entitled man"* to herself.

We walk through the automatic sliding doors and spot him right away. He's wearing a beanie, sweats, and a hoodie in the middle of summer, and is standing at the airline counter.

Does he think he blends in like that? Fucking idiot.

The attendant at the counter gasps when she sees his hands, and we appear behind him. Rio grabs Dustin's shoulders and leans in.

"Dustin, *mi amigo,* what're you doing here? How did you get out?"

Dustin's face turns ashen, and his hands—or what's left of them—begin to shake. "How—"

My hand latches onto his arm. "I'm so sorry, miss. He's not supposed to leave his room. You know"—I lean towards her—"the padded kind of room."

Understanding dawns on her face, and her focus darts between the three of us.

"Wait—No—I—"

I cut off Dustin's protest with a hand over his mouth.

Rio steers Dustin towards the door and calls over his shoulder, "We'll just take him back now. Thanks!"

Dustin doesn't put up a fight until we have him in the car. He thrashes in the back seat and attempts a few swings at me and Rio. Before he can cause any real damage, I subtly slip the syringe from my pocket, stick the needle in his neck, and push down on the plunger. The fight in him dies almost immediately as he slumps down in the seat.

"*Buenas noches.*" Then under his breath Rio mutters, "*El hijo de puta no se aguanta.*"

Son of a bitch still can't take a hit.

CHAPTER 12

RIO

*P*ulling into an empty parking lot around the corner from Euphoria, I open my water bottle and pour some of its contents on Dustin's head. He sputters and lifts sits up. The sun has set, and the club is busy for a Monday night.

Groaning, he lies back down. "Are you two fucking crazy? Taking my fingers wasn't enough? Now you won't let me leave New York."

"You hear that, Z? *Estamos locos.* What do you think?"

Together we laugh low, in a tone that promises chaos.

"There is something wrong with you two . . ."

Zane smiles and shakes his head. "Tell me something I don't know."

Dustin sits up, and tears form in the corners of his eyes. "Just let me go. I don't have anything you want. I told you everything I know."

"*Es ahí donde te equivocas, amigo.*" *That's where you're wrong, friend.*

"Do this one thing for us, and you're free to go. We'll even pay for your plane ticket. You can leave and never look back.

You'll be leaving behind your family, but I get a feeling that doesn't matter much to you, seeing as how you were at the airport without them earlier," Zane says with a shrug.

"Hey! I care about my family!"

"You have an interesting way of showing it," I mumble.

Dustin looks out the window, frustration evident in his voice. "And what if I say no?"

I smile wide. "Well, you still have other appendages I can remove."

Dustin's hands shake, and his pitch goes up. "What do you want from me?"

Tossing the equipment into the backseat, Zane answers him. "We need you to go into Euphoria and wear this."

Dustin picks up the listening device and his whole body trembles. "You can't be serious! You might as well take my fucking arm now because I won't have a damn head if I get caught wearing this!"

I scoff. "Don't be so dramatic.

Zane's mouth thins in displeasure. "We're not exactly giving you a choice here, asshole. Wear the wire, or you'll lose more than your fingers this time."

Dustin's tears have escaped his eyes, and snot drips from his nose.

Aye dios mio. Suck it up.

"You're going to go in there with this wire hidden under your shirt. You're going to ask to talk to Cain. Get him talking. Show him your hands. That and the shiner in your cheek might be the things that save you. See what you can find out about a man named Anthony Cole."

He sobs in the backseat. "I'm a dead man."

Zane's face flushes with rage. "You became a dead man the moment you thought you were above your Oath of Honor. You signed your death certificate when you touched an underage girl."

"I told you I didn't know she was underage!"

Zane shouts over Dustin's whining. "You're dead because of your own fucking choices! Don't look to either of us to save you!"

Neither Zane nor I would even piss on a man like Dustin if he were on fire. Because he wears a badge, he thinks he's untouchable. Fuck that logic.

I'd like to believe that if we weren't here to do something about men like Dustin and Troy, there would be someone else to take up the mantle. But we're here now, and we're willing to make the decision. It's not even a hard one.

Dustin continues crying; I turn in my seat and give him a piercing stare. "Pull yourself together. We don't have all night."

When he makes no move to strap on the wire, I do it for him. He doesn't put up a fight. Instead, silent tears slide down his cheeks.

I should probably feel something for Dustin, but I don't. He deserves what has happened to him.

Zane and I pull Dustin from the car. "All right, asswipe. Walk me through it. What are you supposed to do?"

Dustin shivers in the warm air as he cries. Zane grumbles and finds a scratchy paper napkin in his backseat. "Clean yourself up and walk us the fuck through it."

Wiping his nose and dabbing at his eyes, Dustin shakily responds. "Talk to Cain and dig for information."

"And ask about Anthony Cole," I prompt.

Dustin nods. "Ask about Anthony Cole."

Clapping my hands, I nudge Dustin in the direction of Euphoria. "Now that we're all on the same page, *vamos*."

One foot in front of the other, Dustin trudges away across the concrete.

Zane crosses his arms and leans back against the passenger door. "He's definitely a dead man."

I mirror his stance next to him. "You got that right."

Once Dustin disappears around the corner, Zane speaks up again. "Want to listen and eat snacks in the car?"

"Duh."

CHAPTER 13

ZANE

Everyone makes fun of my car because of how small it is, and that's fine. We'll see who's laughing when we're in a chase and either need to get away, or catch up to a mother-fucker, and we are able to do it because my "clown car" can weave in and out of traffic.

Fuck them.

Rio and I make ourselves comfortable in my car with a bag of cheese puffs and a couple of energy drinks. With our seats slightly reclined and my laptop set up between us, we sit back, waiting for the show to start.

Vibration pulses on my center console. "Is that Spencer's mom calling her phone again?"

Opening the top latch, I snag the phone and read the name "Mom" across the screen, saying, "Yep," then decline the call.

Rio frowns. "How many calls is that? Seven in the last few days?"

"Nine, I think."

"Should we tell Spencer?"

"Not yet. There's something off about her. I'll look into it soon."

"*I fucking hate you for this.*" Dustin's voice crackles through the built-in speaker.

"Right back at ya," I reply, even though Dustin can't hear us. "Do you think we should have given him nicer clothes to wear? Ya know, to blend in."

"Nah. He's fine. We both know the likelihood of him coming out of this alive is slim. A fancy suit wouldn't have changed that."

"Can't argue with that logic."

Dustin's hyperventilating is giving me a headache. I know it's hard for people to accept their death, but this process would be so much easier if he'd just move on.

You're going to die, man. Get over it.

There are a few gruff greetings from what I assume are bouncers and security. Then booming music with a heavy downbeat blasts through my laptop. When the music fades, a deep baritone voice says, "*The boss says he'll speak with you now.*"

"*O-okay.*"

"Pffft. He's going to have to pull it together if he wants to survive more than ten seconds," Rio comments as he munches away on our food.

"Shhhh. We need to listen," I snap back.

A voice, I'm assuming belongs to Cain, says, "*Ah, Dustin, my friend. Good to see you.*"

"*You know who I am?*"

A new voice joins the fray. "*Of course. We never forget a face. Especially one who has been so essential on our road to success.*"

"*Oh. Um. Are you Cain?*"

"*No, no. Cain couldn't be here today. Pardon my lack of manners. I'm Anthony Cole, and this is my associate Pierce Murphy. Come and have a drink with us.*"

"Sure. Okay. That's a cool tattoo you have there. The sk——"

"An impulse decision. Ignore it."

My fingers tap my thigh in a frantic rhythm. "Fuck, I don't know what's worse. No Cain, or Anthony being there."

Rio nods. "At least we know for sure that Spencer's ex is in New York."

There's a clank of glass from the speaker and more conversation.

"Oh shit. What happened to your hands, Dustin? That looks awful." Pierce questions with a chuckle.

"Uh. A work accident."

"That's some nasty accident. How did it happen?"

"I was . . . Umm . . . Chasing a shoplifter, and he came at me with a knife."

Rubbing the back of my neck, I comment, "I didn't realize he was so dumb. A shoplifter? He's fucked."

"You got that right." Rio shakes his head.

"A simple shoplifter did all that? You hear that, Anthony?"

"I did. Shoplifters must be tougher in New York." There's a rustle of fabric, and Anthony's voice comes through louder. *"So, update me, Dustin. How's the little issue Cain tasked you with taking care of?"*

"It's done. No problem at all."

"Good man, Dustin. Cain will be happy to hear it. Now, tell me, where's your partner? Troy, I believe, is his name."

Dustin stutters through his answer yet again. *"He's . . . Uh . . . at home. With his wife. Yeah, it's her birthday."*

"We're not going to get anything. Dustin is useless. There's a reason he's never made detective." A heavy sigh releases from my chest.

"I wonder what the reason was," Rio deadpans.

"Well, thank you for coming in. Cain will be in touch soon with your next assignment."

"Oh. Okay. Th——thank you."

My lips press flat. "Something isn't right."

"*Dustin, before you go, do you know why you were tasked with getting rid of those files?*"

"*No.*"

"*I lost a very prized possession. She slipped through my fingers, and I've been doing everything in my power to get her to make the right choice and come home. She's proven to be more stubborn than I originally believed her to be, but the things keeping her here won't be a problem much longer.*"

"*I—I don't see how——*"

"*I've had my eye on this prize for the last seven years. For four of those, she was mine. So, when my flower ran away to New York, I tore apart this whole damn country looking for her. She took something of mine when she left, and when I finally found her, I kept a close eye, with help, of course; I'm a busy man.*"

"*Uh. Are you talking about art or a——*"

"*Don't interrupt me, you insipid, spineless man. After all my hard work trying to find my missing piece, I wasn't going to let something like a few trivial police reports ruin everything. I have a spotless record, and it needs to remain that way.*"

"*Okay? Well, you're in the clear.*"

"*Yes, I know that. But do you honestly believe that I bought your pathetic story? A shoplifter?*"

"*You need to get better at lying,*" Pierce chimes in. "*But it's too late for you to develop that skill.*"

Another crackle comes through the speaker.

"*Let me go! I didn't tell them anything!*"

"*We know you didn't——you don't know enough to say anything. But now that you've seen us, we can't let you leave.*"

BANG! BANG!

Two shots snap in the air.

"Shit," I mutter.

Rio states the obvious. "Well, he's dead."

"*Can you believe he actually thought we were going to let him leave?*"

Pierce laughs. The sound grates against my nerves. *"Spencer's boy toys obviously got to him."*

"Don't call them that. They're nothing to her."

"If you say so."

"What's that bump under his shirt?" Anthony asks.

A rip of cloth echoes in my car.

"Shit! He's wearing a wire."

"That's our cue." I throw the car into drive and peel out of the parking lot.

Asher isn't going to like this.

CHAPTER 14

ASHER

rewing a cup of coffee, I rub my eyes and accept that the little sleep I got earlier is the only rest I'm getting tonight. Nightmares of Rachel plague me. I used to miss her and how she made us feel. I've mourned her and moved on, but finding her hanging in my closet is a sight that will never leave me.

My body drops onto the couch, and I scan the contents of the coffee table in front of me. Crime scene photos, autopsy reports, and Post-It notes litter the dingy cedar wood. It's like a morbid vision board.

The serial has been quiet, which makes me nervous. A man like that isn't quiet for long. He's escalating his timeline. Pretty soon, his ritual isn't going to be enough.

The fact that we still haven't nabbed him is grating on me. Security cameras are always erased, or he chooses areas where security cameras aren't present. There's never an eyewitness willing to talk to us.

I'm tired of the odds being stacked against us.

Setting my mug on a coaster, I lean forward with my elbows

resting on my knees and notice a few of my notes are on the ground—crumpled. Rio must've accidentally done that.

A creak sounds from upstairs and I angle my head towards the staircase, waiting for another sound. These old houses squeak and creak every ten seconds, making me feel like Casper is going to come and drink a beer with me or something.

I'll do a perimeter sweep in a few minutes and check on Spencer to make sure she's sleeping well. Her sleep quality shouldn't matter to me, but I can't help that it does. I want her happy, smiling, and satisfied from multiple orgasms, given by me. I want her pussy squeezing the life out of my dick while I pound into her . . .

I fucking hate babysitting.

I shake my head, turning on the TV. The local news showcases my least favorite reporter.

Goddamn Sherry Jenkins.

The biggest mistake of my adult life was sleeping with her when I was a beat cop. She didn't disclose that she was a journalist who was only after the scoop on an open case. I tossed her ass to the curb when I caught her digging through my things.

Sherry sits up straight with her blonde bob and navy pantsuit. "Tonight, on Channel Nine, we have breaking news. A serial killer is at large, on the streets of New York City. People are calling him the Bride Butcher . . ."

I groan. "Fuck!"

My phone vibrates on the couch cushion next to me. Hesitantly, I answer. "This is Dawson."

"Have you seen the news?" Kowalski asks.

"I have it on now. Is there another body?"

"Yeah, here in Chelsea."

My stomach drops. Chelsea. Where Spencer lives. Where

Spencer would be right now if the events of the last few weeks hadn't unfolded.

Fate is playing in our favor, but it may not be that way forever.

"You gotta get down here, man." Kowalski pants like he's going to be sick. "It's bad."

My hand drags down my face. "Are you sure it's our guy?"

"You need to see it for yourself. I'll text you the address." He hangs up before I can ask any more questions.

"Shit," I mutter to myself. I can't leave Spencer here alone.

Scrolling my phone, I dial the two idiots who left me to babysit.

"What's up?" Zane's voice spills from the speaker of my phone.

"I got another body."

"What? You had fun without us? And with Spencer there? How does that work?" Rio whines.

"Not me, dumbass. The killer dropped another body. I have to go to the scene. Where are you?" Right when I ask, I hear tires outside, and I peek out the window. Zane and Rio exit the Honda, darting up the steps.

I end the call and wait for them to come inside. Turning towards them, my eyebrows inch upward. "Where's Dustin?"

"Probably fish food by now," Rio explains and takes my spot on the couch.

"What happened?"

Zane approaches me and holds up his laptop in answer. "You can listen and find out for yourself."

CHAPTER 15

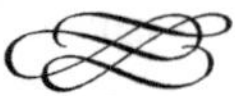

SPENCER

I scramble to quietly dive under our king-size bed. Once again, my ass barely makes it under in time. My head is on the side facing the doorway and I peer through the few inches of space.

Anthony makes an appearance and lingers in the doorway.

"Oh, Floooooower."

A sob threatens to leave me, but I bite my tongue and swallow it down.

His feet carry him to the bathroom. "Clever, Flower. Very clever."

Shit. I must have left the cabinet open.

I squeeze my eyes closed and cover my mouth again. I let out a silent, shaky breath as he knocks around items in the bathroom.

He hasn't found me yet. He hasn't found me yet.

"Hello, Flower."

My eyes bug open, and I finally let out the scream lodged in my throat as Anthony grips my hands and drags me out from under the bed.

When I wake, I'm alone, and silent sobs wrack my chest. My cheeks are wet, and my throat feels scratchy. I sit up, bringing my knees to my chest, and rock back and forth. The motion doesn't bring me any sort of peace, but my mind and body are on autopilot.

I wish they were here.

Darkness blankets the world outside.

I can't believe I slept so long.

A headache threatens to take over, but I ignore it. Releasing the tension from my shoulders, I notice that the blankets are on the floor, my shirt is rumpled, and I no longer have pants on.

Umm. What the hell? Where did my leggings go?

Rio and I spent the day getting lost in each other. It was beautiful and perfect—everything I needed. But I know when we fell asleep in Zane's bed, I had leggings on.

Maybe I kicked them off in my sleep.

You did use a lot of energy in your activities *earlier.*

Ugh.

Rio and Zane's voices float up the stairs, and a fluttery feeling warms my chest. With a pair of sleep shorts on, I head down the stairs when a familiar voice, a voice I haven't heard in three years, pulls me up short.

Stopping at the bottom step, I spot Zane, Rio, and Asher gathered at the bar in the kitchen, huddled together. Anthony's voice streams from the laptop in the middle of their circle, and a chill sweeps over my skin.

"I lost a very prized possession. She slipped through my fingers, and I've been doing everything in my power to get her to make the right choice and come home. She's proven to be more stubborn than I originally believed her to be, but the things keeping her here won't be a problem much longer."

This can't be real. My lips tremble, and a light sheen of sweat coats my cold skin.

The implication is clear.

He's here, and he's not leaving without me.

A whimper slips free, causing all three heads to turn to me. Zane hits the pause button immediately, grimacing.

"What're you doing up, Angel?"

My voice lowers to a whisper. "How did you get that?"

Asher shows no emotion while Rio makes his way to me. He reaches for my hand, but it's too much. I slip out of his grasp and speak more clearly. "How did you get that?"

Rio gulps audibly. "We found him."

"And he just let you walk away? He shot at all of you, for heaven's sake! What made you think this was a good idea?"

Oh my God.

I grip the banister for balance. "Promise me you won't go near him again. Please." I look each of them in the eyes, and they all give me the same look.

They're going after him.

My grip on the banister turns my knuckles white, and blood rushes in my ears.

"Spencer?"

The room fades away as an old familiar one surfaces. Expensive marble countertops, polished tiles, top-of-the-line appliances. The smell of cigars wafting through the air and lasagna in the oven fills my nose.

I'm not there. This isn't real.

"Spencer? Angel? Talk to me."

Glass breaking. Two gunshots.

I'm not there. I got out. I'm never going back.

"Princess!"

My eyes snap open and I'm no longer hanging on to the banister. Instead, two large hands cling to mine. They're warm and rough.

Three large bodies surround me. Three bodies that have done nothing but make me feel safe. Even when I found them in the basement, I knew they wouldn't hurt me.

I've always known that.

"Mama, look at me." A bronze hand with black ink guides my chin to the right to look up into a bright face.

Rio.

"Talk to us."

Tears spring in my eyes. "I can't. I can't go back there."

"You're not alone this time, Angel." Zane's cedar scent drifts to me from my left, and something in my chest settles.

Peering up at Asher, who still has a hold of my hands, I wet my lips and shake my head. "I—"

He drops my hands and takes a step back. "How long are you going to lie to us?" His tone is deep.

"What? I haven't lied about anything!" My pulse increases, and my face flushes.

This frustrating behemoth is going to make me explode.

"You're not telling us everything—or anything at all! If you really wanted to keep everyone safe, then you'd tell us what we're up against." His chiseled jaw visibly tenses.

Explosion incoming . . .

"If you would have let me leave like I had planned, none of you would be in this mess! You can't make decisions for me and then get angry with me about the consequences!"

The vein in his temple pulses. "If you would think things through, then I wouldn't have to make choices for you."

"Ash," Zane cautions.

"No, Z. We all know something happened. She's terrified of him, but she won't tell us why. She has nightmares, and now we know she has flashbacks. If you're that dedicated to helping her, then you need to know—*we* need to know."

Can they actually help me? Is that something I'm willing to accept from them?

Asher turns his menacing scowl on me. "Maybe you should just go."

My heart stops.

This is what I wanted—what I've been trying to do. So why can't I agree with him? Why can't I get the words out?

Because you don't actually want to leave.

"No!" Rio shouts.

Zane balls his fists. "You can't kick her out. We all live here."

"Someone needs to remain neutral when she's the reason everything goes to shit. You two are in so deep that you don't know what's up and what's down."

Asher gathers his gun and wallet from the table by the front door. Before he leaves, he turns his attention back to me. "I have to go to a crime scene. When I get back, be here or don't, but either way, your choice needs to be final."

Zane's knuckles turn white. "You're only leaving because you don't want to be here in case she leaves."

Asher takes a deep breath. "If she wants to leave, don't stop her—she'll only resent you in the end. But if she stays, you better find a way to get some answers. You won't like it if it's me who questions her." With that, the door shuts behind him.

The silence in the room creates a suffocating pressure.

Rio turns back to me, grabs my hand, and caresses it with the back of his thumb. "What's it going to be, Mama?"

CHAPTER 16

SPENCER

My jaw slackens, and I openly stare at the two beautiful men in front of me. They stare back, waiting for the words to come out of my mouth. I know what they want to hear, and part of me wants to say it and believe that we all can be happy together. But the other part of me can't forget Anthony's words or what I know he's capable of.

"I—I—"

Zane's eyes shut, and he turns his head away.

"You're two are just going along with what Asher said? You're going to make me choose?"

Rio squints and takes on a challenging tone. "You told me yesterday that you're mine. Are you taking it back?"

"Ugh! You men are so frustrating!" I push in-between them and stomp to the living room. With my hands on my hips, I stop in front of the TV.

"What's holding you back?" Zane's presence appears right behind me. I want to lean backward into his body and use the strength he gives me.

"You know." I lean my head down and stare at my feet.

Rio's shoes enter my frame of vision. "No, we don't. Asher's right. You haven't been honest."

Fucking hell.

My gaze snaps up, and I narrow my eyes. He's looking back with the same intensity and a glance over my shoulder lets me know Zane's face is the same—scrutinizing and disappointed.

Stepping away from between their bodies, I back away. "I don't owe you answers."

Zane crosses his arms and remains quiet and cold. He's never looked at me like that before.

"Oh really? So, is this how it's going to be? We give and give, and you're going to take without any reciprocation?" Rio's words hit me square in the chest.

Is that what I've been doing?

Possibly . . .

I'm stopped when I bump into a side table next to their large couch.

"That's not what I'm trying to do," I spit back.

"Yeah? Could've fooled me. Did our day together mean nothing to you?"

Ouch.

"It meant everything to me!"

Another glance at Zane tells me he's not going to step in. He started to come to my defense earlier, but the white knight is nowhere to be seen now.

Rio throws his arms out at his sides. "Then prove it! Why are you always so ready to run?"

"Because—"

I can't even say it. I've never had to—never wanted to.

"Because why?" he pushes. "Once again, no reciprocation." Rio crosses his arms, taking up the same stance as Zane.

My nails bite into my palms as I curl my hands into fists. "That's not fair!"

I don't recognize this man—this bitter angry man in front of me. I guess I should've known their patience would run out.

Rio scoffs. "Isn't it, though? I told you everything."

Shame wraps me in its cocoon as I let out truths no one else has ever heard. "And I gave you both what no man has had of me in three fucking years!"

These fucking men!

"Let it out, Mama."

"We're here, Angel."

"Is that what you wanted to hear? That I haven't fucked another man since I left Anthony in Houston? Which I'm sure you know is where I'm from since you did damn background checks!"

They both just nod.

That's it? That's all I get? A fucking nod?

I squeeze my fists and realize they're no longer empty. We all look down at the empty beer bottles in each hand. Rio and Zane smirk like they're twins, and I don't like how my core pulses.

Traitorous, horny body.

My blood boils.

They want to laugh? Fine. I'll make them laugh.

I wind back one hand and let the bottle fly at Rio, and the other soars towards Zane. Each man ducks, and neither bottle hits its target. Instead, they land in the kitchen with a crash and the sound of the glass shattering on the tile.

"Ugh!" Next, I gather the multiple remotes and hurl them across the room. Rio and Zane dodge again.

Why do men think they know what's best? Is it every man, or just the ones I encounter? What is it about controlling me that's so appealing?

Coasters, game controllers, vases, and picture frames make their way into my hands, and I chuck them at the men who are swerving and diving to get out of the path of the inanimate objects. As I launch each item, I continue to let out the truths no one has ever heard.

"He raped me! Is that what you wanted to hear? Anthony raped me while his piece of shit best friend held me down! Pierce laughed the whole fucking time!"

With nothing else to throw, I squat and grip the end of the wooden coffee table. When I push up with my legs, I raise the side I'm holding and shove it forward, sending the flipped table in their direction.

"I shouldn't have to explain that to you! I don't owe you that story!"

The only thing left is a standing lamp in the corner. I grab it with both hands and rip the cord from the wall, then I stalk towards the large TV mounted on the wall and raise the lamp like a bat.

"I'm!"

THUD!

"Tired!"

WHACK!

"Of!"

BANG!

"Controlling!"

SLAM!

"MEN!"

CRASH!

The TV is smashed to bits, and I drop the lamp, but my pounding heartbeat still doesn't settle. Glass and plastic litter the carpet around me. I turn to Rio and Zane, who are behind the couch, still wearing those fucking sexy smirks.

Great. Now I'm angry and needy. How is it possible to feel both?

Their smiles turn feral and Rio taunts. "Come and get us, Mama."

CHAPTER 17

SPENCER

The cry that releases from my throat embodies every moment that I conceded. Every time I did as someone else wanted, and every time I put someone else's needs and desires above my own. All my anger at those who pushed me around, all the anger I have with myself, is finally released from its suppression.

I launch myself toward the men who I both want and despise at the moment. I use the back of the couch to jump to Rio who is standing right there. My legs wrap around Rio's head as I whip my weight around and take us to the floor. We land with Rio on his back and my knees on either side of his head.

Rio stares up at the apex of my thighs. "Shit, Baby, if you wanted my face buried between your thighs, all you had to do was ask."

My right fist aims for his head, but a strong ivory hand wraps around my wrist. "Now, now, this is no way to treat your boyfriends."

The feel of his hand on my skin makes my panties uncomfortably wet.

Not. Now.

"Fuck off!" I grab Zane's wrist with my free hand and twist it to an uncomfortable angle, then roll, bringing him to the ground as well.

We all scramble to our feet and face each other. This time I run for Zane and aim a few blows at this torso. He dodges and blocks each punch. When he strikes, he aims to grab my wrists. I move out of his range, and my back runs into another body.

Rio.

His thick, inked arms wrap around me, trapping my arms. His body covering mine sends a jolt of need to my clit.

Dammit! They've turned me into a sex-crazed woman.

I widen my stance and drop my weight, causing Rio to have to lean forward. Stepping to the side, I wrap my leg around the back of his and push back with my upper half while kicking out my leg. We fall backward to the floor, and I bring my elbow down on his stomach.

The air in Rio's lungs rushes out, then he rolls on top of me, but before he can trap me underneath his body, I lean forward and lace my fingers together behind his neck. When I throw my weight back down, I thrust my hips upward and send him rolling over my shoulder.

I jump back up to my feet, positioned with my back to the front door. If I don't choose them, then now is my time to go—this is my opportunity.

But once again, my feet don't move.

Fucking hell.

I guess this is my answer.

It always was.

Damn Snarky Spencer.

"You never should've pushed me to tell you something I wasn't ready to tell you."

Zane shakes his head. "You could have told us from the beginning. Did you think we'd think less of you? Think of you as weak?"

I bite my lip.

"You're the strongest person I know, Angel. To live with that fear, that memory, every day and still choose to make a life and live . . . I'm in awe of you."

A mewl slips free.

Damn Zane and his beautiful words.

Rio takes a few steps towards me. "Spencer, we're here. We weren't there before, when you had to deal with this all on your own, but you're not alone anymore. We're here, and we aren't going anywhere."

It's like they can see into my mind and are addressing the list of insecurities and fears that have been swirling around in there for years.

Why do these men have to set my body on fire and melt my heart at the same time?

Zane steps towards me now. "I know what it's like to be afraid every day; to worry in every situation what might happen. To want to run at every turn but have that thing, or that someone, that holds you back."

Rio holds a cautioning hand out. "Z . . ."

"Total honesty, right?"

Rio nods and gives Zane an encouraging look.

Shit. I don't know if I'm ready to hear this. But this isn't about me, it's about Zane. Another man who has been strong for me, and he deserves the same in return.

"I grew up in the foster system in New Jersey. My foster parents, Teresa and Michael, never should've been approved to foster children. They were evil. They would lock the pantry and fridge—only giving my foster sister, Sarah, and I food when we were 'good.'" He flexes his hands and continues. "And they had friends who liked young children. Their friends would pay them to spend time with Sarah and I."

My lips tremble and my hand covers my mouth.

"They had one who called me his favorite. He'd come over, and they'd lock me in my room with him. At first, we'd just play games. Then the games became . . . different."

My head shakes rapidly.

"I know you've wondered why I couldn't handle your hands on my back that night, but you've been too shy or kind to ask."

I force my voice to come out normal and not give away that I'm barely keeping it together. "You don't have to tell me, Zane."

"I want to." He swallows and blinks a few times. "He used to force me onto my stomach and hold me down. He was bigger and stronger, so it didn't matter how much I fought. He always got what he wanted in the end."

"Zane." My voice breaks.

Zane lets out an angry laugh. "I wanted to run away so many times. I could have done it and survived, but I couldn't leave Sarah. She was so young and so pure, there's no way I could have ever left her in that house."

I feel pieces of my heart breaking with every word from Zane's mouth. What he's been through . . . no child should have to endure.

"Z, you're not to blame for—"

"I know!" Zane takes a deep breath. "I know that. I wasn't even ten years old when Sarah died. One of Michael's coworkers got a little too rough with Sarah one night. The asshole didn't realize she couldn't breathe. I tried calling nine-one-one, but Teresa told them I was just causing trouble, and they left. She hit me so hard that I blacked out."

My vision blurs, and my cheeks suddenly have tear streaks.

"I packed my backpack full of food that I stole from the kitchen and ran as soon as I woke up. When I was caught, I was placed in a different home. Teresa and Michael claimed that Sarah had run away too. No one believed me when I tried to tell them what happened."

No one? Not a single adult in his life would listen? All these people were supposed to protect him, love him. They let him down in the worst way. They hurt him and used him. The system that was set up to keep him safe failed.

My breathing grows ragged as my stomach clenches with the force of my restraint. I've never wanted to hurt someone so much in my life. I want to make Zane's foster parents hurt the way they hurt him. I want them to know what it's like to feel small and powerless.

"Are . . . did they . . . Teresa and Michael . . . do they still have kids?" My hands shake as I struggle for the right words.

Zane gives me a sympathetic smile. "No, Angel. They're not foster parents anymore. They're not anything anymore."

I scrunch my eyebrows. "But . . ."

"I killed them. It took me years to face them again, but when I did, they didn't survive. I killed them, and I've killed others like them. I've seen too much to feel sorry for my actions, Spencer. I'll never apologize for killing people like that. Teresa and Michael may not have touched me, but what they did enabled those bastards to do it—to take *people* and sell them. I'm not sorry I put them down like the animals they were. We are the Devils of New York—the few who fight back."

I shouldn't be surprised. These men—my men; my *boyfriends*—they're brave. I shouldn't be surprised that they have the courage to face those who have caused them and others pain.

"I'm so sorry. Can I—"

"Yes, Angel. Of course."

I run at Zane and jump into his arms. He catches me as I wrap my arms and legs around him, enveloping him in comfort and love.

Zane leans his head back to look at my face. "Are you staying, Angel?"

Through tears, I answer, "Yeah, I'm staying."

"Thank fuck." Zane's lips meet mine, and his tongue immediately invades my mouth. Another hard body crowds me from behind, and lips make their way down my neck.

"Say you're ours, Mama."

Rio's hands grab my hips. His fingertips trace up my sides and grope my full breasts.

I moan. "I'm yours."

"Good because there's no way in heaven or hell we would have let you walk out that door."

CHAPTER 18

SPENCER

Rio grinds his hard length into my ass while Zane presses his between my legs. I moan into Zane's mouth as our bodies move together in a sensual dance.

I take one arm and hang on to Rio's neck. Rio sucks on the tendon between my shoulder and my neck, causing me to break my kiss with Zane and moan. It's all too much and not enough at the same time.

"We're going to fuck you right here, Mama. *Si no estás de acuerdo, dilo.*" *If you're not okay with that, you need to speak up now.*

A flush overtakes my skin. "Please."

"Good girl," Rio growls in my ear, then looks to Zane.

A mischievous smile spreads across Zane's face. He drops my legs and commands, "On your knees, Baby."

Looking up at him, I lower onto one knee and then the other. His fingers lightly caress my chin. "You look so perfect just like this—on your knees, between us. Ready to be fucked."

My panties dampen, and I squirm. I need them. I need their hands, their mouths, their cocks.

My eyes drop to the bulge in his pants and lick my lips.

"Is that what you want, Angel? You want my dick down your throat?"

I nod my head desperately.

"Then take out my cock." Zane's focus jumps to Rio. "On your knees. Find out how wet Spencer is."

I unzip Zane's pants and pull out his thick, hard cock and stare. I don't know how this thing fit inside me the other day. *Shit.* And now I'm getting even more turned on by the thought of giving him head.

Dear God, please don't let me make a fool of myself.

I brace my hands on his thighs and lick him base to tip, swirling my tongue around the head. I savor Zane's pre-cum as his salty taste explodes across my tongue. He groans, and the muscles beneath my hands tense. Feeling more confident, I take him in my mouth and suck, bobbing my head back and forth.

"Fuck yes. Just like that," he growls.

Rio drops behind me and pulls my leggings and panties down to my knees. His hand cups my pussy, and his middle finger dives between my slit. His finger easily explores my pussy with how wet I am.

"Our girl is soaking my hand," Rio reports to Zane.

Zane hums his approval. "Slip a finger inside her. Just one."

Rio obeys Zane's order. His finger slips in my core and begins pumping in and out. His thumb circles my bundle of nerves while he whispers in my ear, "You're doing so good sucking him down like that, Baby."

As Rio whispers more filthy words in my ear, I take Zane deeper into my mouth. When he hits the back of my throat, I gag and pull away.

"Breathe through your nose and relax," Rio urges. But it's hard to focus when his thumb starts flicking my sensitive flesh back and forth quickly. The pressure in my core builds faster than I thought possible, and I moan around Zane's cock.

"Give her another finger."

Rio doesn't hesitate to do as he's told. When the second finger is added, he finds my G-spot and gives it attention. I'm immediately enraptured. I lean back into Rio's body, Zane's length slipping from my mouth with a pop, as I cry out my climax.

My muscles are still twitching when Zane lowers himself to his knees in front of me. "Hands and knees, Angel. I'm going to fuck your pretty mouth while Rio fucks your perfect pussy."

Rio lifts my shirt up over my head and puts a hand on my back, urging me to lean forward. When I comply, I eye Zane's glistening cock, and Rio removes the rest of my clothing swiftly. Whispers of clothing sound around me as Zane and Rio remove their clothes.

I watch as Zane takes off his shirt in a swift motion, revealing his chiseled abs and a delicate tattoo across his ribs. It's like his body was cut from marble by Donatello himself.

"Are you going to let me fuck your face, Angel?"

My mouth drops open in shock. Every time he speaks, it's a shock. More like a shock to my libido, but a shock nonetheless.

"Yes," I reply. My voice is breathy and full of want.

Zane grabs his hard cock with one hand and traces my jaw with the other. "Open up, Spencer."

As Zane enters my mouth, Rio slowly pushes into my core. My body is in sensory pleasure overload. Being filled by these two men is everything.

"Fuck, you take us so well," Rio praises as he moves in and out of my pussy.

Instead of waiting for Zane to move, I move for him. I bob my head up and down, taking his length as far into my mouth as I can manage. Tears stream down my cheeks, and I look up at Zane through wet lashes.

Zane gazes down at me, lust filling his eyes. "My perfect Angel." He gathers my hair in his fist and guides my head with his hold. I'm a mess as drool drips from my chin. I should feel embarrassed, but the way Zane looks at me makes me feel empowered and cherished.

All of our moans swirl together as the inferno of sensations grows.

"If you don't want to swallow, tell me now, Angel. I can't hold back much longer."

Instead of answering him, I double my efforts.

"Spencer!" Zane shouts as my mouth fills with his cum.

Rio leans forward and speaks into my ear with a husky tone. "Come with us, Baby." He pinches my clit, and I explode. My muscles contract around Rio's cock and my whole body shakes with the rush of pleasure.

"Fuck yes, Spencer. Milk my cock dry."

Our ragged breaths are the only sound in the room. My legs almost give out from under me when Rio lays on his back next to me and pulls me down with him. Zane grabs a blanket from the back of the couch and joins us on the floor. I nestle my head on Zane's chest as Rio secures his body around mine.

Rio peppers my shoulder with kisses and Zane plays with my hair, and my muscles relax with their show of affection.

I trace six inked butterflies that lay across his abdomen.

"They're for Sarah."

My heart clenches.

"She died when she was six. She loved butterflies, so I stole butterfly clips from the store to put in her hair with her braids."

Zane continues to amaze me.

I lean over him and kiss each winged creature. "She was

lucky to have you, Zane." My chin wobbles as I kiss his cheek and settle back down against him.

Rio kneads the knots in my back and Zane continues running his fingers through my hair. When my mind is at the edge of consciousness I hear, "I love you, Angel."

"*Te amo, mi corazón.*"

I love you, my heart.

ASHER

The flashing lights from the squad cars hurt my eyes. I don't care how many times I've been around them; the seizure-inducing dance of lights makes me want to punch things.

Ducking under the crime scene tape with a coffee in hand, I walk down the damp, dark alley between a bodega and a bookstore in Chelsea.

"Took you long enough."

"Calm your tits, Berkowitz. I got here as fast as I could."

His tie is loosened, and the top button of his shirt undone. His hair looks like it was once styled neatly but has since been tousled.

He runs his hands through his thick, dark mane and breathes a deep sigh. "It's bad."

I hand him my paper coffee cup and make my way around the side of the dumpster. Kowalski stands there, looking down at the sheet covering the dead body. He remains still, with his lips pursed.

"Did the M.E. come by?" I ask, shaking him from his concentration.

"Not yet; they're on their way. Busy night, I guess."

I snap on a pair of gloves and squat down, moving the sheet back to examine the scene.

I've seen a lot of ugly in my time with the bureau, and even before then with NYPD, but the pure rage displayed here, makes my stomach churn. I can't focus on how her eyes are empty. I can't think about how the bruises on her body stand out like a sore thumb. I can't wonder about what was probably going through her mind when the piece of shit raped and killed her.

My feelings need to take a back seat while I examine the body—not woman—objectively.

The wedding dress is covered in blood and torn; her face is unrecognizable. And instead of one purple hyacinth, there's a whole bouquet scattered and ripped apart.

My voice comes out detached, just like I need to be. "The state of the gown suggests he dressed her before he killed her, a deviation from his MO. There's a sticky substance here that looks to be semen—another deviation. He's usually careful. Make sure the crime scene techs swab it. And the damage to her face, along with everything else, suggests he's devolving."

Berkowitz nods in agreement as Kowalski briefs me. "I searched her for an ID and didn't get one. We'll have to rely on DNA or dental records for identification."

Berkowitz crosses an arm and rests his chin in his other hand. "There's more than one flower this time, and he tore them apart. His anger at the target of his affection is growing. He's always been reverent with his victims, showing remorse and taking the time to lay them out. He either isn't able to get to the one he wants, or she hasn't given him the recognition he's seeking from her."

"Or both," I add.

Kowalski pulls out his notepad. "I talked to a local florist; purple hyacinths aren't easy to come by in the summer. They usually bloom in the spring. He has to be ordering them from someone, or he grows them himself."

"Good work." I drop the sheet and mentally count the days in my head. "His cooling off period is getting shorter, which means we're probably going to have another body soon."

"Or there's one already out there that we haven't found yet," Kowalski speculates. "This guy is going to be bigger than John the Baptist thirteen years ago."

Berkowitz gives a derisive snort. "No way. John the Baptist killed twenty-four women in less than a year."

Leaving them to their debate, I stand from my hunched position, and a few pops ring out from my knees and hips. I groan and lightly stretch. I look down again, and the dispersed hyacinths cause another sight to flash in my mind.

Spencer shocked and terrified as she held a vase of flowers.

The vase broken and bits of glass all around the kitchen.

Ah, hell.

"When we get the possible DNA sample from the dress, have the techs compare it to the sample we got from the NYPD."

"On it," Berkowitz answers.

"And has anyone talked to Marreli?" I inquire.

Berkowitz and Kowalski glance at each other then me.

Shit.

"Fine. I'll take this one, but the next call comes from one of you." I raise my phone to my ear and wait for my supervisor to answer my call.

"You better have a lead, Dawson," Marreli says groggily.

"I have a theory."

CHAPTER 20

SPENCER

ealizing my presence is no longer a secret, I look up and catch Anthony's gaze. His pretty blue eyes are not the warm ocean breeze I know them to be, they're sharp as ice. Specks of red dot his face and clothing. His mouth pulls up into a grin. Beside him, Pierce chuckles.

"You should have knocked, Flower."

Cold sweat coats my skin as I lie there on the king-size, memory foam bed surrounded by a fluffy comforter and Rio's warmth. I take deep breaths and soak in the security Rio's arms bring me.

When I fell asleep in Rio's room earlier, it was still light outside. Zane, Rio, and I were eating Chinese takeout while watching the *Twilight* movies because Zane had finished the last book and I insisted he watch the movies. It was entertaining to see his and Rio's reactions.

Asher had been out all day today working, I assume.

Rio's arms are still wrapped around my torso and his face is nuzzled in my hair as he breathes deeply. Zane accidentally woke me up when he slipped from the bed a couple hours ago. He had a gotten a call and needed to head into work.

A shout rings out in the quiet house—desperate and full of terror.

"No! This can't be real!"

What is going on out there? Please don't let this be another basement incident.

Slipping out of Rio's hold, I tiptoe into the hallway on quiet feet. The shouting continues, coming from up the second flight of stairs. When I reach the top, I peek in the only open door.

It's another bedroom with metal and brick accents, black curtains, and a large bed in the center with onyx bedding. But the comforter is askew as Asher tosses and turns in his sleep in the center of the bed. The little moonlight from the window reflects off his sweat-soaked skin, and I can hear his breaths coming in short bursts.

He's wearing a pair of boxers and nothing else. With the lack of clothing, I can see the colorful ink decorating his arms. In the dark, I'm able to make out a dragon swirling down his right arm. On his left he has a large tree spanning the width of his bicep. The colors dance and complement each other beautifully.

"Please! Someone help her!"

My heart breaks for him—trapped in his own mind. I'm too familiar with the feeling.

Just because I'm mad at him, doesn't mean he deserves to be left alone at a time like this.

"Rachel, please no!"

Who the hell is Rachel?

Cautiously, I approach the side of the bed where he lies with his back to me and run my hand down his arm.

Apparently, that was the wrong fucking move.

He grips my wrist and, with little effort, pulls me over his body and lays me flat on my back. He's on top of me in less than a second, his knees straddling my hips, his hands gripping my wrists above my head.

"Asher!"

His eyes are open, but he doesn't see me—he hasn't come back yet.

"ASHER!" I yell again.

When he still doesn't hear me, I bring my heels up to my butt and buck my hips up, causing Asher to fall forward and let go of my wrists. Immediately, I wrap my arms around his torso and trap one of his arms in my hold as well. He goes to break my grip by attempting to push away. Asher is stronger than I am, but I'm faster. Before he can get free, I buck my hips again and roll us to the side, ending with me on top.

He grabs my hair, but I slap him across the face before he can pull. The slap echoes in the room, and Asher pauses. Afraid I've hurt him; I softly stroke the cheek I hit. The skin there is covered in stubble.

Timidly, I ask, "Asher? Are you okay?"

His grip on my hair loosens, and he covers his eyes with his hand. "Did I hurt you?"

"Wha—"

He clenches his jaw. "Don't lie to me."

"No." My answer is rushed.

He sits up easily, even with my weight on top of him, and leans back against the headboard. "You shouldn't have come in here."

Instinctively, I want to shrink away from his rejection but pushing me away is his shield. We all have that innate impulse to protect ourselves—it's literally hardwired into our brains. Asher is no exception. Right now, I'm a threat. He's vulnerable and doesn't want to show me his fears.

He was my rock when I couldn't breathe after Anthony sent

me the flowers. He doesn't understand how essential he was in that moment. I felt safe enough to break down, he should get the same.

"You were there for me when I needed someone."

He still won't look at me. "I was just doing my job."

"Is that all I am? A job?" I do my best to not let the hurt leech into my voice. He's hurting and trying to push me away. I need to prove that I don't scare so easily.

When he refuses to answer, I decide he needs a push . . . or a distraction.

I place a hand on his chest and bring my face close to his. "Do you make everyone you care for in your job come?"

He sucks in a breath. "That was—"

I drag a finger down his chest and allow my eyes to wander lower. His abs are perfectly sculpted and there's a light smattering of hair across his pecs. "A mistake? Try again. You're not dumb, Asher. You don't make impulsive decisions. If I was truly a mistake, you wouldn't have tried to touch me again the next night."

He fists the sheets next to my legs and finally looks me in the eye. The intensity there makes my skin tingle, and I rock my hips.

"Stop it," he says through clenched teeth.

The big bad Viking doesn't want to play? Too bad.

I quirk my brow. "Stop what?"

"Don't play dumb, Princess. You know exactly what you do to me."

Splaying my hands over his chest, I drag my core back and forth against his hardening cock. "I don't know what you're talking about."

I have no clue where this bold woman came from, but I'm drunk on the power. I love seeing how I affect him. Me; I make this man hard. I make him want.

"Is that what you want? You want to hear how you make me crazy? Fine." His hands grip my hips, and he thrusts his hips upward, putting the perfect amount of pressure on my clit. "Just the thought of your tight, little body drives me insane. I'm not sure whether I want to spank your ass raw or kiss you until you can't breathe."

My thighs squeeze together, and I moan when he hits that spot again just right.

"Is that what you want, Princess? You want me to slap your ass over and over as I drive my cock into your pussy until you scream for me?"

I whimper then bring my mouth to his and let him devour me. His tongue invades my mouth, and I moan louder.

His hands roam my body, and all thoughts drift away. All I can think about is how I need his hands and mouth everywhere.

I should be strong. I should stick to what I said before.

You know . . . that's not a bad idea.

Grabbing his wrists, I slam them against the headboard on either side of his face. Then I pull away and tease. "No hands, remember?"

"You're still going with that?"

"I told *you* 'No hands.' I didn't say anything about my own."

With a cocky smile, he links his fingers behind his head. "You want to touch me, Princess?"

"Yes." My voice comes out needy.

"Then touch me."

Deciding to draw out the torture, I glide my hands over his chest and allow them to travel south. I tease the skin right above the waist of his boxers. "Where can I touch you?"

"Anywhere."

Arching a brow, I grow bolder. "What if I want to go lower?"

His eyes go wide, shocked at how I'm taking control, and he gives a small nod. He parts his legs, and I move to the space between them. I pull his waistband down and his cock springs free.

Holy shit. What did I just get myself into?

He's huge. I'm embarrassed to admit that I'm not as experienced as the women I'm sure he's used to. Anthony is the only man I've ever been with until recently, and I don't want to bring that up now. He doesn't deserve space here.

I keep the insecurity off my face when I grab Asher at the base and give him a few firm strokes. He hisses and drives his hips into my hand.

Tossing my self-doubt aside, I ask, "What if I don't want to use my hands either?"

He pauses and smirks. "As you wish, Princess."

Narrow my eyes, I chide, "You really need to stop calling me that." Then I lick the underside of his shaft. He groans loudly, and my nervousness disappears.

I've only done this a handful of times before, but I find that I enjoy this with Asher. And I want to explore more.

Running my tongue across the tip, his cock jerks and I smile. I continue to lick slowly until I have him begging. Wetness floods my panties from my core as I revel in his taste.

"Open your mouth, Baby."

I can't answer him, so I just quirk my brow.

"Please, Princess."

My core grows wet, so I open and take as much of him as I can into my mouth. His tip bumps the back of my throat, and I gag.

"Breathe through your nose and relax your throat."

Determined to make him wild, I do as he says, and the tip of his cock slips past my gag reflex. My head bobs up and down in his lap as I suck him in and out. His moans grow deeper, and I peer up at him through my tear-lined lashes. He's looking at me like I'm the most beautiful thing in his world. My heart swells as tears leak out of the corners of my eyes. I may be on my knees, but I'm in charge.

I release him with a *pop*, grab his hand, and bring it to the back of my head. "Fuck my mouth. I want to choke on your fat cock."

"Shit. You're perfect, Princess." Then Asher gathers my hair in his fist and tugs, guiding my mouth back down toward his hard length. He drags his tip across my bottom lip, and my tongue slides out to get another taste of him and lap at the bead of precum.

"Are you sure?"

My head snaps up and I look him directly in the eye. "Shut up, Asher." Then I dip my head and take him all the way to the back of my throat.

Asher's hips snap up impulsively. "Shit." He pounds away in my mouth, making it almost impossible for me to keep up, but I keep sucking and licking which continues to make him go crazy. I rub my thighs together, seeking any amount of friction, but I'm still left wanting. Tears stream down my face as I look up at him again.

"Are you wet, Spencer?"

Unable to give a verbal reply, I nod.

"Then reach into your panties and touch your needy pussy."

Slipping my hand inside, I find myself dripping. My fingers glide right through my folds. I flick my clit and let out a breathy moan.

"That's it. Keep going. Use your fingers to make yourself come."

Doing just as he says, I plunge two fingers inside my core and quickly find that spot that never fails to quickly bring me to the edge.

"Tap my thigh, Baby, if you don't want me to cum down your throat. This is the only warning I'm giving you because that perfect mouth has me so fucking close."

In answer, I squeeze his thigh with my free hand and double my efforts. Before I know it, ropes of cum are jetting out of him, and I do my best to swallow them down. At the same time, my release hits me, causing my whole body to tense and shake from my orgasm.

When I've swallowed the last drop, Asher lifts me up his body. "Damn you and your sexy as fuck mouth." Then he slams his lips to mine and tastes himself on my tongue. I moan into his mouth and kiss him back with all the pent-up emotion I've suppressed for days. His hands go straight to my ass and grip it hard.

The kiss is lazy and lust-drunk. Eventually, I slow down and pull away. Biting my lip, I glance to the side. "I didn't like that look in your eyes."

"What look?"

Tears form again and take a deep breath to keep them at bay. "Pain."

Asher's grip turns rough. "Is that what this was? A pity blow job?"

Matching him, I aggressively clutch his shoulders. "You know that's not what this was. Don't take this moment away from me because you're scared."

"I'm not scared," he snaps back.

I raise a challenging brow. "Then tell me who Rachel is."

His whole body tenses and he shuts his mouth.

"That's what I thought. Now, hold me." Rolling off him, I

tuck my body into his side, and he wraps an arm around me while pulling up his boxers with his free hand.

Knowing he's still feeling vulnerable, I give him a bit of truth to even the playing field. "I've never liked giving head before, so thank you for making it a good experience. Well . . . except with Zane . . . But . . . Never mind."

He makes a muffled sound against the top of my head. It sounds like something between disbelief and a growl. "I don't know if I should punch your ex or return the favor."

A small smile tugs at the corner of my mouth. Up until now their protectiveness has been inconvenient, but I'm getting used to it. "Neither is necessary, big guy." Taking a deep breath, I offer more of myself to ease him. "I have nightmares too. It's nothing to be ashamed of, but I get it. The memories take something from you every time and leave you wrung out."

Asher turns his body towards mine and pulls me closer, so my body is flush with his, my head resting on his muscled chest. His heartbeat echoes in his chest and relaxes me. He begins playing with my hair, brushing it out with his fingers.

After a few moments, I drift off to a blissful sleep, free of Anthony and free of my horror. But one thing I can't let go of is the truth this man is hiding.

CHAPTER 21

ASHER

Fuck me. This woman is too good to be real. At her core, she's kind and thoughtful, and I don't deserve her tender love and care.

I jerk my hands away from Spencer's body, and she stirs in her sleep.

My hands—these hands—they don't deserve her soft curves. I may not regret the lives I've taken, but I know my actions mean I don't get to bask in the peace she brings me.

Silently, I slip out of my bed, immediately feeling the loss of her warmth. I take one last moment to drink her in—this brave woman who brought me out of the dark when I was drowning in my nightmare.

I slip on a pair of gray sweatpants and head downstairs. When I get to the kitchen, I find that I'm not alone. Rio is there with a cup of coffee in hand. He raises a brow in my direction, but I ignore it and pour myself a cup even though it's two in the morning.

"You two weren't very quiet," he comments from behind his mug with a smile.

"Shut up, dickhead," I snap.

"I'm just saying, for someone who claims they don't want her—"

"Drop it," I growl and lean back against the countertop, taking a sip of my coffee.

Rio raises his hands in surrender, still holding his mug, and keeps smiling. "Okay, okay. Consider it dropped. But . . ." His smile drops. "Be kind."

"Huh?"

"You gave her an ultimatum, so consider this mine. Don't lead her on. If you insist on keeping your distance, then you need to do just that."

I clench my jaw. "She came into *my* room tonight."

"Did you suddenly lose the ability to say no?"

Like I could have said no when I woke up with Spencer on top of me. Then she made her way down my body and . . .

Ignoring his point, I switch subjects. "What did you learn about Anthony? I've been busy with the shitshow left for my team by the fucking *Bride Butcher*—I hate that name."

"Well . . ." Rio trails off as his eyes wander to the side.

I narrow my eyes. "Please tell me you actually got answers."

"She's definitely staying."

We'll see.

"And . . ." I prompt.

"We know Anthony raped her."

I set my mug down harder than necessary. "We all already guessed that! How is that news?"

"Now we know for sure." Rio casually shrugs.

I pinch the bridge of my nose and squeeze my eyes closed. "Do I have to do this myself?"

"You're being dramatic."

"We need more. There's more she's not telling us." I down the rest of my coffee and set my cup in the sink. "When everyone is up later, we're going into the office—together. It's time Spencer stopped hiding behind her fear and gave us the truth."

I don't care how beautiful she is, and I don't care how she effortlessly draws me in. Spencer needs to give us some damn answers so I can keep my family in one piece.

CHAPTER 22

SPENCER

Sitting in an FBI interrogation room is not how I thought today was going to go. When I woke up alone, in Asher's bed, I wasn't surprised he didn't stick around for the awkward "this can't happen again" conversation.

But when I woke up to the smell of pancakes and bacon, I did not expect for Asher to say that we were all going to work with him. He made it very clear that I, specifically, didn't have a say in whether or not I went. So, I got dressed and when we arrived, Asher placed me in this room with a glass of water and left.

That was an hour ago. Maybe longer.

I don't mind quiet—I prefer to spend time in my own company. But with nothing to do except stare at these walls and a two-way mirror . . . I might go crazy.

My mind has already replayed all of my most embarrassing moments, and all of the times I should have said something different. Like yesterday, when Rio surprised me in the shower and I made the most ungodly and humiliating sound. It was like a cross between a donkey baying and a cat screeching.

Now, I'm just staring at my reflection and wondering what the fuck is going on. I didn't do anything wrong, so I assume I was left in here so I'm out of the way. But then that begs the question: Why do I need to be here in the first place?

The metal chair is cold, and I swear they keep the temperature below fifty degrees in here. The LED light overhead buzzes and is finally starting to get on my nerves. Keeping my eyes open is getting more and more difficult.

Right when I'm getting ready to settle in and take the world's most uncomfortable nap, Rio walks in.

"Seriously? What the hell!" I lean back in my chair.

Rio winces and shuts the door behind him. "Sorry." He's wearing a suit and tie today and there's something about seeing him all dressed up with his tattoos peeking out above his collar that sends a fluttering through my stomach.

"Aren't you supposed to be my lawyer? Wouldn't a lawyer make sure I'm treated fairly? Not to mention the fact that you're my boyfriend?" I give him a pointed look.

Rio's eyes widen, and a charming smile stretches across his face as he strides to me. "Did you just call me your boyfriend?"

"Uhh . . ." I didn't think he'd catch that, but that's what I agreed to, right?

He peers down at me. "Say it again."

My eyes dart around the room. "Boyfriend?"

His rough hand turns my chin in his direction. "Next time, say it like you mean it, Mama." Rio leans down and slams his mouth to mine in a passionate kiss. Even when the door opens and someone clears their throat, Rio doesn't pull away.

"That's enough, Rio. We have shit to get done."

When I open my eyes, I look up to see Asher with his hand on Rio's shoulder, pulling him away from me. Zane is gazing at Rio and me with a heat in his eyes. My cheeks flush knowing Zane and Asher saw Rio and me going at it.

I really need to chill.

Oh God. They really have turned me into a sex-crazed monster.

Or was she always there?

Fuck Inner Spencer and her horny ways.

Rio pulls up a chair and sits next to me while Asher takes a seat across from us. Zane leans against the wall next to the mirror with his ankles and arms crossed. The feel of the room goes from playful to formal and slightly claustrophobic.

Am I on trial here?

Asher sets a thick brown file on the table, and I hear a crinkle of paper come from next to me but just out of my sight. "Ms. Gray—"

"Ms. Gray? Is this a joke?"

Ms. Gray, my ass. He wasn't calling me Ms. Gray when I fucking had his dick in my mouth last night.

Asher gives me a stern look. "Ms. Gray, let's start with something easy." He reaches down and pulls out a clear plastic bag with a red piece of tape that reads "evidence." He sets the bag on the table and asks, "Have you ever seen this before?"

My eyes widen. In the bag is my handgun. I glance to my side for guidance from Rio.

"You don't have to answer that."

Asher gives Rio an exasperated look. "Not helping, man."

Rio shrugs. "My priority is my client. I'm advising her not to incriminate herself. That gun is a class D felony and we both know where you got it. Ms. Gray here could earn up to seven years in prison. I wouldn't be a good lawyer if I didn't intercede on my client's behalf."

Asher breathes an exhausted sigh. "Fine. If your client provides useful information, the potential gun charge will be dropped."

"In writing," Rio says with a smirk.

Asher groans and leaves the room.

My jaw clenches. "Was he really going to charge me with a felony?"

Rio shakes his head.

I frown. "Then why are we going through all the motions?"

Rio leans to the side and tilts his head to speak to me. "Mama, I'm a lawyer. I learned early on that you cross all your T's and dot all the I's—you can never be too careful. The government is sneaky and knows how to sway a jury."

"Sway a jury? This wouldn't have gone to a jury, right?"

Rio gives a noncommittal shrug. "You never know. The law isn't black and white like everyone thinks. It's all about what you can prove, or convince the jury of. A prosecutor would have no problem persuading a jury that you knowingly bought this gun illegally and were fully aware that the serial numbers had been filed off."

I throw my hands up. "But you said Asher wouldn't have charged me."

"He wouldn't. I can't speak for his partners or his boss."

That shuts me up.

After about twenty minutes of waiting, Asher comes back with the paper Rio requested, signed by Asher's boss, Aaron Marreli. Rio looks it over, then slides it to me with a pen. I scribble out my signature and hand it back to Asher.

"I would like a copy for my records," Rio tells Asher.

Asher deflates in frustration. "Seriously, man?"

"You can never be too careful."

"Whatever. I'll get you a copy after." Asher's attention turns back to me. "Ms. Gray, have you ever seen this gun before?"

I cross my arms and peek at Rio, who gives me a nod of approval. "Yes."

"Is this your gun, Ms. Gray?"

Another peek, another nod. "Yes."

"Where did you purchase the gun? There's no official record of the sale, so I'm assuming you bought it from someone illegally."

When I peek at Rio for a third time, Asher makes a sound of annoyance. "You don't have to look to him for everything."

I put on my best brat face and reply, "Excuse me, I'm consulting my lawyer." Rio nods again. "I bought it from a guy in Central Park. My ex-fiancé terrifies me, and I needed a way to protect myself without there being a paper trail."

Asher leans on his arms on the table. "What was the name of the seller?"

Shaking my head, I give him an answer he doesn't like. "I don't remember."

"Oh, come on." Asher rolls his eyes.

"I'm being honest. I don't remember his name. It was an old guy name, though—I know that much. I remember thinking it was odd his mother named him that and figured it must be a family name."

Asher squints. "Hank?"

I snap my fingers. "Yes! That was his name. Hank."

I'm unable to see Asher's face when he turns to Zane. Zane doesn't seem phased, so everything must be okay. "I know."

Asher rights himself in his chair and inquires, "Have you heard of the Bride Butcher?"

Receiving another nod from Rio, I tell the truth. "No."

Asher sighs. "You're not in trouble here, Spencer—you have the paper to prove it. You don't have to look to Mr. Flores for every answer."

"Could've fooled me, Mr. Dawson," I mock. "Since we're in an interrogation room, this seems like the perfect place for questions. Where did y'all get that recording of Anthony?"

"Hold that thought," Asher instructs and gets up from his chair.

"Leaving when the questions get tough? Hypocrite," I mumble.

Asher raises a brow. "I'm going to turn off the recording equipment. There are some things that we don't need a record of." He leaves for a few minutes and comes back to his chair quickly. He waves his hand at me. "Okay, throw your tantrum."

I place my hands on the table and stand. "Tantrum? Bullshit, Mr. I-Have-A-Badge. You three must have done something incredibly stupid to get that recording. Now, what was it?"

Asher stands and matches my position. "*I* didn't do anything."

My brow furrows. "Huh?"

"It wasn't me. Ask them." He points to Rio and Zane.

"You've got to be kidding me." I pinch the bridge of my nose.

"We can explain, Angel." Zane crosses the room to me.

Sarcasm and vexation leak from my every pore. "Oh, goodie. Please do."

"Dustin Cox wore a wire—"

"You mean Police Officer Dustin Cox? Was he undercover?"

Rio interjects into the conversation. "Well . . . it wasn't exactly voluntary."

"What do you mean?" My lips purse.

"They're talking about coercion, Princess." Asher rests his hands on his hips.

I look down at Rio, still sitting in his chair. "Why would you force him to wear a wire? Is he okay?"

"If you consider a bullet in his brain okay, then yes. *Está bien.*" *He's good.*

My hands fly to my mouth, and I gasp. "You killed him?"

Zane shakes his head. "No, not us. Anthony. We made him

wear a wire and go to a strip club to talk to people to get information on Anthony."

My head spins, trying to make sense of it all. "Y'all are talking in circles."

Zane grabs me by the shoulders and turns me to face. "Dustin wasn't a good man. We found out what he did and used that against him. We made him wear the wire, dropped him off at the club, and listened in on the conversation. Anthony wasn't happy and killed him. That's all."

My head feels like it's stuck in a vise. "This is too much. I'm done here. Let's go." I turn to leave, but Asher grabs my arm before I can make it to the door.

"We're not even close to being done here. You still haven't fulfilled your end of the deal."

"Are you shitting me? What other information could I possibly give you?"

Asher leads me back to my chair and takes up his on the other side. "If you're going to be childish about this, fine." He flips open the file and begins pulling out photos, each just as horrid as the next. He lays out six photos depicting dead women lying on the ground.

The blood drains from my face as my eyes scan the pictures with numbed horror. "They . . . They're all . . ."

"Dead." Asher's voice is empty.

"Wearing my dress."

Zane rests two hands on the table, Asher stares in a catatonic stupor, and Rio's face turns stricken. The pin-drop silence bounces off the walls as everyone stares at me. I'm even sure whoever is watching on the other side of the glass is staring.

All my men recover at the same time.

"What?"

"What the hell, Angel?"

"Are you sure?"

My stomach hardens into a tight ball, and I'm pretty sure I stop breathing. "That's my dress. My mom helped me pick it out after Anthony proposed. And they're all holding . . ."

"Purple hyacinths."

Asher gives me a sympathetic look. I knew Anthony was always looking for me—his text messages indicated as much—but I didn't think he'd go this far.

I lick my dry lips. "Are all of them from New York?"

Asher points to each photo in order. "Austin, Texas. Evergreen Falls, Idaho. Willow Creek, Wyoming. Brooklyn, New York. Los Angeles, California. Oakland, California." He reaches back into the file and pulls out another photo. This woman is unrecognizable. Her face is beaten and bloody, and the hyacinths are cut up and scattered around her body. "Harlem."

Delicately grabbing the photo, I examine it closely. "Anthony used to buy me hyacinths after we got into an argument, or after he'd hurt me. It was always little things. When I pushed the wedding date back the first time, he grabbed my arms so hard that I had bruises for over a week. I never thought of myself as an abused woman—he never punched or slapped me, so I thought it didn't count, and I was too ashamed to show my mom."

Rio's hand wipes a tear on my cheek that I didn't know was there. "There's nothing to be ashamed of here."

I give him a half-hearted smile, not entirely sure I believe him. Turning back to Asher, I continue. "It didn't happen often, but when it did, he'd buy me purple hyacinths. He always said his flower deserved flowers and that purple hyacinths showed how sorry he was. But the next day, the flowers were always ripped to shreds." I place the photo back on the table and cross my arms.

"That's not creepy," Zane murmurs sarcastically.

Asher gathers the photos and places them back in the file. "Do you know where he'd buy the hyacinths?"

I shake my head. "No, I don't. I'm sorry." I fidget with my hands in my lap. "What were their names?"

"Angel . . ." Zane rests a hand on my shoulder.

"I need to know."

Asher shakes his head and gives me a pitying look. "I'm not telling you their names; it won't help anything."

My body goes numb. "I feel responsible. If I had just gone back to him when he texted me the first time, maybe those women would still be alive."

"Don't do that to yourself, Mama. It's not your fault. There's no way you could have known. He might have still done it even if you stayed." Rio grabs my hand and gives it a squeeze.

They're too kind—they'll make every excuse to make me feel better. But how can I not feel responsible? He's doing all of this because of me, because I won't go with him.

"But that's just it. I should have known. I should have! Especially after I saw . . ."

Asher leans forward in his chair. "Saw what?"

I bite my lip and glance to the side.

Asher uses an index finger to guide my chin back to him. His eyes are soft and distressed. "After you saw what, Princess?"

"After I saw him kill someone."

CHAPTER 23

SPENCER, SEVEN YEARS AGO

I walk across the cold, checkered tile floor. Even wearing shoes doesn't keep the cold from seeping into my bones. It's everywhere—it bleeds from the walls. No matter how many sweaters or socks I wear, it doesn't matter, I always have chills. They constantly run up my spine and make the hairs on the back of my neck stand on end.

He likes to keep the house at a brisk sixty-nine degrees, which should be perfect for Texas summers, but in this house, it keeps me on edge. I can't explain why.

I have the perfect life. The perfect fiancé, the perfect house, the perfect job.

Maybe it's the little things Anthony says here and there. He made a comment about watching what I eat the other day and has been more hands-on about what I wear when we go out. I've been with him for just over four years; he's never cared about that kind of thing until I moved in six months ago. That's when things changed. He got more cagey, more picky. I'm pretty sure it's because he has an issue with one of his clients. He makes a lot of people a lot of money. Dealing with hundreds of thousands, and sometimes millions of dollars would stress out anyone.

I've heard him yelling more and more in his home office lately—like now.

I know he's stressed, and he always tells me I'm his ray of sunshine. So tonight, I'm determined to be his sunshine and make his life a little brighter. I'm making his favorite meal—homemade lasagna with breadsticks and salad. And for dessert, another favorite, peach cobbler. I always cooked for myself and Mom growing up, so cooking dinners when I moved in was no big deal.

Making my way up to the second floor, his voice booms down the staircase.

"You fucked up! You fucked up so bad there's no coming back from this!"

Anthony has a voice that naturally carries. I tense when he raises his voice, but there's nothing he can do about that. He can't help that he's so loud.

He's ruthless at work which just makes him better at his job. He does it all for me, to provide for me. To give me the life I didn't have with Mom. He even provides for her sometimes too. She needed help with her water bill last month and he paid it without question.

"I-I'm sorry Mr. Cole. I can fix it. The shipment can be salvaged." The fear in the man's voice is unmistakable. My own fear mixes with his as my muscles tense in my back, but I continue to push myself forward.

Wait . . . shipment? But Anthony is in stock trading. Maybe he's helping a client with something?

My steps slow and goosebumps break out over my skin as I push myself to keep walking.

"I don't think he's actually sorry." I pause at the new voice. Pierce Murphy. I didn't know he was here; I didn't see his car in the driveway. I'll have to put out another place setting for him. If Pierce is here, at this time, he usually stays for dinner.

The man has made me uncomfortable from day one; the way he watches me, the way his eyes roam my body. But he's Anthony's best friend and they work together, so he can't be all that bad.

I can't help how my smiles turn fake and my stomach knots at the thought of having to spend another evening with him.

Biting my lip, I inch my way to the grand double doors with ornate gold handles. Hopefully a kiss and the promise of his favorite meal will be enough for Anthony's stress to alleviate.

"N-no. I'm sorry. So sorry. This will never happen again. I promise, Mr. Cole. Never."

Is the man crying now?

Depressing the thumb lever, I open the door with silence. Anthony likes the house to be kept in pristine condition, so the door doesn't even squeak when I open it.

I stop halfway through the door and my hand grips the door handle harder than before.

What the hell is going on here?

There is a man on his knees on the cherry wood floors and he's staring up at a handgun that is leveled at his head. Make that two handguns. One in Pierce's hand, and one in Anthony's. Pierce and Anthony's backs are to me, and I think the man is one of Anthony's employees, but it's hard to tell because his face is beaten to hell. He has cuts actively dripping blood down his face and one eye is swollen shut. Who did that to him? Was it Anthony?

"Goddamn right it won't happen again," Anthony says nonchalantly. Ice runs through my veins at his calm voice. He seems so relaxed, but the tick in his jaw says he's anything but.

Maybe the gun is just a threat.

But then Anthony nods to Pierce and they squeeze their

triggers in unison. The double *boom* bounces off the book-shelves lining the walls and rings through my ears.

I can't stop the audible gasp that escapes my mouth. My free hand shakes as I watch the blood stream from the two holes in Henry.

One in the heart. One in the head.

The lifeless eyes burrow into my soul and eat away at the happy bubble I was living in.

Realizing my presence is no longer a secret, I look up and catch Anthony's gaze. His pretty blue eyes are not the warm ocean breeze I know them to be—they're sharp as ice. Specks of red dot his face and clothing; his mouth pulls up into a grin. Beside him, Pierce chuckles.

"You should have knocked, Flower."

Before Anthony can say anymore, I turn and flee. My feet are no longer quiet on the hardwood floors, and I don't care.

"Oh, Floooower!"

I run through the living room and entryway, straight for the front door and fumble with the keypad. All the exterior doors have keypads on the inside and outside. My hands don't stop shaking as I type in the four-digit code.

1-7-2-1

But the light still blinks red.

1-7-2-1

I pull viciously on the door, but it doesn't budge.

"That door won't work, Spencer." Anthony's voice comes from the top of the stairs.

I flip around with my back pressed to the thick white door. My breath rapidly heaves in and out of my lungs, threatening to pull me into unconsciousness.

I can't let that happen.

I try to focus, darting my eyes around for the next exit, I mentally decide on the exterior door off one of the guest bedrooms down the hall, towards the back of the house. I don't want to go by the stairs where Anthony is probably descending —probably to kill me.

"We just want to talk," Pierce calls out.

Shit. Shit. Shit. They're both coming.

Pushing off the front door, I spring down the hallway. My heartbeat is in my ears as I pump my arms. I dart into the first room and go for the French door. Each guestroom has a four-poster queen bed with simple yet comfortable bedding, an exterior door, and an updated en suite. Anthony pushed me to update the guest rooms when I moved in. He wanted me to make the house my own.

Panting and trembling with adrenaline, I type in the code again.

1-7-2-1

Still locked.

What the hell?

In the next room, it's the same.

Did he change the code? How? When?

Footsteps echo down the hall, and I force myself to think fast. I open the closet, the bathroom door, and curtains. Hopefully it'll make them think I searched the room and moved on.

Praying I fit, I lie flat on my stomach and squeeze under the wooden bed frame. My ass barely makes the cut, but now I'm tucked away with my head at the foot of the bed. Laying my cheek to the carpet so I can see in the two inches of space between the bed skirt and the floor, I cover my mouth with my hand and attempt to slow my speedy breathing. It's impossible, but I have to try, or they'll hear me. Then who knows what will happen next.

I don't want to find out.

A pair of brown leather Oxfords come into view as they

stroll into the bedroom. "Spencer, dear. Come out, come out wherever you are."

Pierce.

There's no way in hell I'm coming out from under the bed.

He paces back and forth in front of the bed, less than a foot from where I hide. He throws things around in the closet and does a quick check of the bathroom. "She's not in the second guest room but definitely came this way."

How are they talking to each other? Shit. I need to get out of here.

I left my keys in my studio above the garage which is through the kitchen and off the laundry room—on the other side of the house. If I make it over there, I can get through a window in my studio and to my Jeep in the driveway.

Waiting until I can no longer hear Pierce's footsteps, I inch out from under the bed. With my heart in my throat, I lean my head out the open doorway cautiously and look both ways down the hall. The *tap tap tap* of footsteps comes from above me and I assume Pierce is on the second floor.

I ignore the quiver in my knees and take measured strides down the hallway.

"Flowerrrrrr." Another round of chills zips up and down my back at Anthony's call for me. "Floooooower." His voice comes from upstairs, but I can't tell from where exactly. I compel myself to move again even though my mind is screaming at me to go back to the safety under the bed.

Maybe I can hide there and eventually they'll give up and leave.

Fat chance. Anthony and Pierce are like sharks. They will do anything to close a deal. I doubt that kind of focus just goes away.

At the end of the hallway, I pause and open my ears, scanning for noise.

A *clank* rings out from the second floor.

Desperate to believe they're both back in Anthony's office, I creep through the living room and kitchen. Every step brings another wave terror. Terror at the thought of being spotted. Terror at the possibility of making an accidental noise.

I jump and a scream almost escapes me when a crash of thunder shakes the windows along the back of the house. Allowing my gaze to wander above me, I check for any signs that they heard my almost shriek.

A flash of lightning casts light on the second floor and I see a reflection in the window of a figure outlined on the balcony right above me.

My fiancé smiles wide as he says, "Gotcha."

Breaking out into a sprint, I pass the scratchy, gray fabric couches and white coffee table in the living room, then the marble counters and the marinara and garlic aroma in the kitchen.

The French door to the laundry room is glass and will do nothing to hide my presence. Even with the lights off in there, the space is still partially illuminated by the kitchen lighting. The storm outside helps hide the moon, but it only aids so much in dimming its light.

I just pray I make it in there before he gets off the last step.

"You're not going to get far, Flower!"

Throwing open the French door, it bangs on the wall and bounces back as I dart across the tile. The heavy door now blocking my way to the garage offers me sanctuary. But when the sound of Anthony making his way down the stairs in the living room makes it to my ears, I freeze. My body locks up and I can't breathe.

Shit. This is not happening right now.

Hoping this plan works twice, I open the garage door all the way and fit myself inside the laundry dumbwaiter. I shut the cabinet behind me seconds before Anthony tears through the laundry room.

"She went through the garage."

"Probably going up to her studio," Pierce replies.

They're both in here. My heart rate doubles, and a stab of anxiety goes through my gut.

Will they find me? Will they shoot me like they shot Henry?

One to the heart. One to the head.

Two *creaks* come from the metal transition when they each step on it and cross into the garage, but I don't dare let out a breath just yet. I wait and count to thirty before I grip the rope and use the pulley to move from the laundry room to the master bathroom on the second floor.

This is the only thing in the house that has yet to get an update and requires someone to use the pulley system for it to move. Thankfully, it's silent.

I jolt and halt when another *"Flowerrrrr"* echoes through the house. Forcing a deep breath in my lungs, I get moving again.

He hasn't found me yet. He hasn't found me yet.

I chant the mantra over and over, praying it's true.

Making it to the top, I open the cabinet, step out, and search for my next hiding spot.

I won't fit anywhere in here. The cabinets are all full, and the shower has a glass door. On light feet I go into the bedroom I share with Anthony. The door is ajar, but no one is in sight.

"You check the library again at the end of the hall. I'll check the bedroom."

Fuck.

I scramble and quietly dive under the king-size bed. Keeping my eye on the door, I take up my post, looking for either of them.

Anthony makes an appearance and lingers in the doorway.

"Oh, Floooooower."

A sob threatens to leave me, but I bite my tongue and swallow it down.

His feet carry him to the bathroom. "Clever, Flower. Very clever using the dumbwaiter."

Shit. I must have left the cabinet open.

I squeeze my eyes shut and cover my mouth again. A silent shaky breath releases from my mouth.

Scanning the bathroom, he knocks around items in his search.

He hasn't found me yet. He hasn't found me yet.

"Hello, Flower."

My eyes bug open, and I finally let out the scream lodged in my throat as Anthony grips my hands and drags me out from under the bed.

He grabs my hair at the crown of my head and lifts me to my feet. I hold on to his wrist in an attempt to ease some of the pain radiating across my scalp.

"You shouldn't have run," Anthony spits in my face.

"No! Let go!" I get my feet under me and kick in the one spot I know will hurt him the most—right between his legs. Anthony groans and falls to his knees, freeing my hair.

With Anthony blocking the doorway, I turn and run for the window, my only escape. I'm sure I can jump in a way that won't injure me too badly.

I wrench open the window as rainwater flows onto the carpet. Bracing my hands on either side of the sill, I step up.

But before I can make it out, a hand snags my foot and pulls me backward. My legs slip out from under me, and my head crashes into the glass. Bile rises in my throat as the room spins. Blood slides down my cheek from the top of my head.

Anthony grips my hair again. "Now look what you did! You're a mess!" He turns with his hand still in my hair and drags me out of our room.

"You're hurting me," I whimper as tears roll down my face. "Please stop."

"There's the little troublemaker." Pierce's smile is too wide when he sees me at the top of the stairs. He's waiting at the bottom next to the buffet table that sits behind the couch.

I trip as Anthony forces me down the steps, but he doesn't stop to allow me to right myself. Instead, he drags me by my hair the rest of the way, and I cry out harder.

"Please, honey. It hurts."

Anthony doesn't even spare me a glance. "Good. Let this be a lesson." He drags me right by Pierce and into the kitchen. My scalp is on fire as he holds on firmly to my hair. I couldn't stop the tears even if I wanted to.

His hold loosens and he throws my head at the tile like I'm nothing more than a ball that will bounce right back up. But I don't bounce back. My head meets the ceramic tile with a crash, and I see stars. My vision threatens to go black, but I fight to stay conscious.

"P-please don't hurt me. I'm sorry. I'm so sorry."

"Old Henry said the same thing, but he wasn't really sorry." Pierce looms over me.

I scramble back in a crab walk until I hit the front of the oven.

"Spencer, Spencer. What am I going to do with you now?" Anthony has his gun out now and waves it around.

My sob brings his focus back to me on the floor. He casually saunters over to me and crouches down so he's at eye level with me. "If you weren't my Flower, I'd kill you right here. Right now."

He uses the barrel of his gun to move hair that had fallen in my face. I freeze when I feel the cold metal drag across my skin. "You need to learn your place. Over the last few years, I let you roam and be free. I let your petals dance in the wind. But the time has come to understand that your place is at my side, and being by my side means I'm in charge. You do what I say, when I say."

My mouth goes dry, but I still force the words out. "Okay. I will. I promise. I won't say anything."

"Not good enough, Flower." He shakes his head at me and scratches his forehead with the barrel. "What were you doing in my office?"

He aims the gun at my head, and I struggle to turn my thoughts into words. All I'm able to do is stare at the small black hole in the center.

"I would answer his question, Flower." Pierce flourishes his gun to the side. He looks way too happy watching the scene in front of him.

"You don't call her that!"

Pierce holds his hands out in a placating gesture. "No problem, man. Just you."

My mouth flops open and closed. "I was coming to tell you dinner is ready." Snot mixes with my tears.

Anthony stares me down like he's trying to find the lie. But there's no lie. If he would just look in the oven, he'd find the lasagna where I left it to keep warm.

"I swear. I made your favorite."

"Just like a good little wife." Pierce laughs.

"No more going in my office." It's not a request. It's a demand. He's letting me know his word is law, and I better fall in line.

I nod my head violently, hoping he interprets it as enthusiasm. Right now, I'm praying that agreeing with anything he says will keep me safe. That's what they say to do in the movies, right? Play along.

Pushing my luck, I turn over onto my knees and crawl to him. "I promise. No more going into your office."

"Do you want to know why we shot him?"

Shaking my head, I swallow the lump in my throat and answer him. "No. It's none of my business."

"Damn right, it's not." Pierce appears next to Anthony.

"You're going to have to prove it to me, Flower."

Dread floods my heart. "H-how?"

"I'm so glad you asked." Anthony smirks down at me then turns. "Pierce."

In a flash, Pierce lifts me up by my arms. He pulls me over to the countertop and slams me down on the cold marble. My head spins when it makes contact, and my breath is knocked out of my lungs.

I move to sit up, but Pierce holds me down by my shoulders. Kicking out my legs, I squirm and try to break free of his hold.

Anthony undoes his belt as he approaches me. The clink of the buckle echoes in my ears and draws my attention.

He's hard.

Oh God. Please no.

"What are you doing? Anthony! Stop!" I already know the answer, but this can't be what I think it is. He's a good man. A loving man.

"You're going to give me exactly what I want." The zipper is loud and reveals his red silk boxers with the head of his dick poking through.

I thrash with more vigor, but Pierce holds firm.

This isn't right. This isn't the man I know.

"Stop moving!" A sting rushes across my cheek as my head is thrown to the side. I gasp in pain, and a metallic taste floods my mouth.

"I said to stop moving!" A gun is thrust into my mouth, and I freeze. Sobs freely leave me, along with more salty tears.

Anthony leans down and licks the side of my face. "This is happening, Flower."

The gun leaves my mouth, and another slap on my other cheek forces my face to the side. A knife cuts my clothing to pieces, revealing my skin.

"You're going to be with me forever."

Thrust.

"You're going to have my children."

Thrust.

"You're going to do anything and everything I say."

Thrust.

"You're going to marry me and be my good little wife, giving me this cunt whenever I want it."

Thrust.

A laugh reverberates above me through the room.

Laying there, I just take it. I listen to every command and nod my head when told to do so. Silent tears track down my face, enraging Anthony further.

I have no power here. No control. There's nothing I can do but lay here while the man I once loved chips away pieces of my soul.

Each motion in and out breaks the purity of the love I thought we had.

If I lie here and just take it, maybe he'll let me go. Maybe this will be it, and I can forget tonight ever happened.

When Anthony is done, Pierce goes to take up his spot.

No no no no no. I can't do this again. No. Please no.

"What the hell do you think you're doing?" Anthony shoves Pierce away from my limp body.

Pierce lifts his hands in a placating gesture. "Sharing in the spoils."

"She's mine! Back off! If you want to fuck something, use your hand or go help break in our newest shipment."

Pierce's face turns red with fury as he stares down Anthony. When his anger turns to me, I attempt to cover up my ripped clothing. He gives me a wink and leaves.

Anthony lifts me and tosses me on to the floor. My head ricochets against the tile. The nausea in my stomach finally comes up and coats the floor. I'm unable to move with all the aches and pains screaming throughout my body.

"Don't bother coming up to our bed. You can sleep here on the cold floor and think about what you did. I don't want to punish you, but flowers have to learn their place."

CHAPTER 24

SPENCER

 y muscles involuntarily shake, and my cheeks are damp with tears. Zane is kneeling next to me, stroking my hair and whispering soothing words. Rio is holding one of my hands in both of his.

Asher is staring at me, and the look on his face promises death. The case file in front of him has taken the brunt of his anger—it's clutched in both of his hands and wrinkled to hell.

"I'll kill him," Asher snarls.

I shake my head violently. "You can't go near him. You can't. And I don't think you should say that in a federal building, especially when you're a federal employee."

"Angel, none of us will lose sleep when we kill that motherfucker."

The sound of my pulse reverberates in my ears. "When?! You said when!"

Rio's cheeks flame. "Yeah, Mama. When. That man's life ended when he laid his hands on you."

I throw my hands up in frustration, even though their show of protection makes me feel needy. "That was before we met!"

When did I become a woman who could be led around by her vagina?

"Then he's been a dead man walking for a long time." An air of warning fills the room.

My face turns into an effigy of infuriation. "You can't just go around killing people! Just because I didn't walk out the door doesn't mean that I'm okay with that!"

Asher places his hands on the table and stands, forcing me to strain my neck so I can stare him down. My eyes wander his solid frame as he rolls up his sleeves. "You think I care about the people we've killed? You think I've lost sleep when I imagine how the life left their eyes? Think again, Princess. We kill those who don't deserve to breathe. I'll never apologize for killing my first supervisor when I found out what he did to the female agents during their 'interviews.' Or how I strung up the team lead who liked to take the child abuse cases just so he could traumatize those kids further because 'the scared don't talk.'"

I cover my ears. "Stop!"

"Ash." Zane cautions Asher with a hand in the air.

"What? Can't handle the truth and how tainted it is? Don't like that the world isn't full of fucking sunshine and rainbows?"

I pound my fists on the table and stand, mimicking Asher's position. "I, just as much as anyone, know the world isn't sunshine and rainbows. Don't throw that in my face."

"Then stop acting like it's all so simple. It's fucking not."

I hate that I get it. I hate that I understand why they are the way that they are. I understand why they're okay with taking lives. Does that mean I'm a bad person?

Maybe it means you're understanding and have a better grasp on right and wrong.

"I hate you," I seethe at Asher.

He smirks, setting my panties on fire. "No, you don't."

I grab his tie and yank him across the table. He leans in, and his mouth finds mine like a heat-seeking missile. Our tongues duel, fighting for control. His hands cup my face, and he angles my head, deepening the kiss.

Asher breaks the kiss and grits out, "On the table, Princess."

I glower at him. "Or what?"

Asher grins. "Oh, Princess. I don't think you want to find out."

Smiling challengingly back at him, I quip, "Try me."

Asher looks to either side of me and nods his head. Before I can ask what's going on, I'm lifted and laid out on the table. Asher has my wrists secured in his hand, Rio holds my hips down, and Zane moves to stand between my legs, which are currently hanging off the end of the table.

"You should have listened."

I watch the men around me, not a single prickle of panic to be found. Instead, there's a fluttering low in my belly. "I think I'm doing just fine."

"Let's see if you feel the same way when you're screaming because of us." My pants and thong are ripped down my legs, and my shirt is lifted above my head and wrapped around my wrists, tying them together. The bitter cold of the metal table bites into my skin.

"The things we could do to this sexy body," Zane claims as his fingers trace the slope of my neck.

Zane grabs a chair and settles in. His head dips, and breathes in my scent, groaning loudly. "Perfection." His deep voice makes my inner muscles clench.

I try to close my legs, but his shoulders prevent me from hiding my center from him.

Rio bends down and begins kissing and sucking my skin

across my stomach and slowly makes his way up to my breasts. "I could spend all day playing with these."

"Please," I whine as I arch my back.

"What did I say to you before, Mama? You never have to beg."

Asher remains by my head and watches the scene playing out in front of him. I can't help but do the same, watching these men worship my body like I'm a queen. Their queen.

A moan escapes me as Asher grabs the other chair and makes himself comfortable. "Your sounds are mine, Princess." Then he captures my lips with his own and drowns me in a kiss full of bliss. His tongue enters my mouth at the same time Rio pulls the cups of my bra down and sucks on my stiff peaks. Asher reaches a hand down for my other breast and rolls my nipple.

Rio bites the side of my breast, and I scream into Asher's mouth. "I'm going to mark you every time, Baby. Every damn time."

My body writhes as Zane kisses his way up my inner thigh. He laves at my clit over and over. Each flick of his tongue makes the pressure in my core build. His fingers delve into my pussy and pump in and out.

The pleasure is too much, yet I need more.

"Please, don't stop," I beg.

"I'll never stop, Angel. Not when you taste this sweet."

His words vibrate against my clit, making me squirm.

When I moan, each man goes back to playing my body like a fucking fiddle. Zane's tongue in my pussy, Rio's mouth on my mound, biting and licking, and Asher's hands plucking at my stiff peak.

"Shit, shit, shit," I chant as I claw at my bindings. The electricity of ecstasy pumping through my body causes my back to bow off the table as pleasure crescendos and overtakes my senses.

"You come so pretty for us, Mama," Rio whispers in my ear.

I sigh when my bra is righted, my thong and pants slide up my legs, and my shirt is adjusted back over my frame.

I didn't know I could be so content. I didn't know this kind of happiness was possible in this life. But being here surrounded by these men—my men—I feel my troubles slip away, one at a time.

CHAPTER 25

ASHER

I really hope I don't get fired for that. But if I do, what a way to go. I'll never be able to question a killer in there again without thinking of how amazing Spencer sounds. I could listen to her come every day, and it would never be enough.

I was supposed to remain the impartial one—the distant one—so I could have a level head when all of this inevitably goes to shit.

It always goes to shit.

Good things don't last for men like us.

But what we just did, I'll hold on with both hands until this thing we have going on turns to dust.

I run the back of my index finger down the side of Spencer's face as she lies blissed out on the table. "I have a few things to wrap up, and then we can head home."

Spencer smiles up at me. "Okay, sounds good. But is there a more comfortable place to relax? This table sucks."

Rio chuckles. "Asher has a couch in his office. You can lie there."

Zane and Rio walk Spencer in the direction of my office while I head the opposite way to Marreli's office. I knock twice on the closed door.

"Come in!"

When I enter, he's typing away at his computer with his glasses resting on the end of his nose. Aaron Marreli is a hard-working agent who, unfortunately, gets stuck with a lot of paperwork. He'd be more useful in the field, but after he was shot in the leg by a bank robber, he rides the desk. He's in his late fifties and probably not retiring anytime soon. His dark hair is peppered with gray, and his face has minute traces of smile lines and crow's feet. He's not a cheery man, but he's fair.

I take a seat in one of the two barely padded chairs in front of his desk. "I just finished my interview with Spencer Gray. I'm pretty sure her ex, Anthony Cole, is our guy. I wouldn't be surprised if he tried to take her again soon. DNA still hasn't been run yet. The lab is backed up. But I'm sure the DNA Ms. Gray got from her attacker will match the DNA from our latest crime scene."

"How did you make the connection?" He pauses typing and looks up from the screen.

"The flowers. Purple hyacinths aren't that common."

He rests his elbows on his desk and steeples his fingers. "Good work. Stay on Gray. You are to be her shadow. I don't want her to so much as sneeze without you knowing. I agree that Anthony will try for her again. I want you there with her when he does."

Fuck, he's right.

Back to babysitting duty.

"If you need a team or to rotate watch, you have the green light."

My head snaps up. "Not necessary, sir. I got it."

Over my fucking dead body will someone else protect what's mine.

Marreli's eyes widen slightly, letting me know I've possibly given away too much.

"Ms. Gray can stay at my house. Kingston lives with me, so between the two of us, we'll have eyes on her twenty-four-seven."

He doesn't need to know that Spencer has already been living with me for the last several days, and that there are multiple reasons why she's safest with us.

He nods and waves a hand in dismissal. "Update your teammates and get back to Ms. Gray. I have a feeling you won't be waiting long for Cole to make his move."

Not liking the truth in his prediction, I rush back to Spencer and my friends, sending a text to Berkowitz and Kowalski on the way.

Rio, Zane, Spencer, and I are all crossing the lobby before long. Spencer was passed out when I got to my office, but she woke right up when I informed them of my conversation with Marreli.

As we approach the exterior glass doors, I spot multiple camera crews lying in wait outside.

"Zane, run ahead and get your car. I don't care who you have to cut off or what laws you have to break. Be fast," I instruct. He gives me a single nod and bolts out the doors. "I don't like this," I mutter.

Spencer's unease rolls off of her as her eyes dart between the news crews and me. I don't offer any empty reassurances—that's not who I am—and I need her on her toes. If she's alert, then she's more likely to stay safe.

After only a couple minutes of waiting, Zane's car pulls up to the curb. "Stay behind me, Princess. No matter what, don't let go of my shirt until we're in the car."

She pushes out a short laugh. "I really wish you'd stop calling me that."

I grin. "I don't believe that." I turn to Rio and switch. "You take up the rear when we exit, then get in the front seat after we enter the car. Are you packing?"

Rio lifts his shirt to reveal a Glock and a couple of knives. "Always. Which, by the way, I'm missing a few knives. Did you take them?"

How he got those through security, I don't want to know.

"No, I didn't touch your goddamn knives. And that's not important right now." I tilt my head towards the crowd outside. "I don't think they're here for us, but . . ."

"Hope for the best but expect the worst," Rio finishes for me. "But really, if you took my knives, just tell me. I won't be mad . . . Maybe."

"Oh my God." I roll my eyes and ignore Rio as he babbles on.

Zane exits the car and stands by the back door, waiting for us to come to him. He eyes each of the people with cameras and microphones with skepticism. He gives me a nod, and we rush out into the noisy New York air.

As soon as we step outside, to my left, Sherry Jenkins steps out from behind a cameraman and gives me a vindictive smile. Her pristine, bright yellow top makes her stand out in the crowd. She taps the cameraman, gestures to me, and struts right to us. As she walks, her greedy gaze zeroes in on Spencer.

Ah shit.

Sherry and her cameraman stop us in our path. "I'm Sherry Jenkins with Channel Nine News. Ms. Gray, how does it feel to be the fixation of the serial killer, the Bride Butcher?"

Spencer's mouth opens and closes in shock, and I step to the side to block Spencer from the camera.

"Out of the way Sherry," I snap. My comment comes out

of my mouth a little too loudly, catching the attention of the newscasters and camera crews. They rush over immediately, but Sherry doesn't pay them any attention.

Instead, Sherry's focus turns to me. "Agent Dawson, you have yet to catch the killer terrorizing our city. Do you have any comment on that?" She shoves her microphone in my face.

I push the mic away. "My only comment is that you need to get out of the way. You're crossing a line."

Sherry smiles and drags a finger down my arm. My skin crawls. "I'm just doing what any good investigative reporter would do."

"Harassing kind, innocent people?" I bite.

"Giving the citizens of New York the truth." Her smile is sinister.

"By endangering the lives of others. Sounds just like the leech you are. Now if you'll excuse me, I have *real* investigative work to do."

Zane finally reaches us and moves people aside. I grab his hand and he pulls us through the crowd. Camera shutters click and flashes litter the atmosphere as we cross the sidewalk. Reporters shout more questions at us, but none of us answer.

Zane shoves Spencer and I into the backseat while he and Rio jump into the passenger and driver seats.

"Go!" I shout, and Zane burns rubber as he peels away from the curb.

"How the hell did they find out so fast?" Rio questions as he pounds his fist on the dashboard in front of him.

Turning in my seat, I watch the crowd behind us disappear. "I don't know, but I plan on finding out."

Only three people knew about Spencer's connection to the case. Once I find out which one it was, they'll meet the devil inside when he comes out to play.

CHAPTER 26

SPENCER

The circus outside the FBI was a shock, to say the least. That fucking woman and the way she touched Asher. I could have wrung her neck. The audacity!

It's not like she knows y'all are together . . . if that's what you want to call it.

Now is not the time to define what Asher and I are. If we even *are* anything at all!

And who the hell came up with the name the Bride Butcher? Probably that dumbass bitch, Sherry.

Too much is racing through my mind to make sense of everything. Zane went down on me in the fucking FBI building, Anthony has been out there killing women because he can't find me, and the news is going to plaster my face everywhere as the cause of the current killing spree in New York. Not to mention my hiatus from work and the fucking exhibit I should have been working on this whole time! If I get back to the studio and my to-do list has become so impossibly long that it has its own zip code, one of these guys will get punched in the face.

Now we're all in the living room watching some ESPN while the guys debate statistics of various basketball players who are retired and compare them to current players. It's all stupid, in my opinion, because it's almost impossible to compare when the game is clearly played differently now than it was then. Which the people themselves have pointed out!

I'm ready to jump out of my skin when Rio and Zane start debating on their own over who would win in a one-on-one: Stephen Curry or Ray Allen.

I pop off the couch and stomp into the kitchen, where Asher is busy making us dinner. He places a tray of chopped, seasoned potatoes in the oven and turns his attention to some marinating chicken breasts.

"Anything I can do to help?"

Asher peeks over at me. He has a kitchen towel hanging on his shoulder, his sleeves are rolled up, and his suit jacket is resting on the back of a chair. "You want to cook?"

"Not really, but I'm going crazy just sitting around. If y'all would just give me my phone back, I could get out of your hair." I sigh.

He turns to the stove and begins cooking the chicken in a pan. "Not happening, Spencer. We're monitoring it for texts from Anthony. He's gone silent since the last dead body turned up."

I move to stand next to him and lean back against the counter. "I have other reasons for needing my phone, especially now that I'm staying."

"If there's anything pressing that comes up, we'll let you know."

I let out an exaggerated groan. "I'm bored and going crazy."

"Read a book." His concentration stays on the pan.

I cross my arms. "I don't want to read a book."

He raises a brow at me. "Do you know how to relax?"

"No."

He laughs. "I figured."

I don't know when the last time I "took a break" was. That phrase isn't even in my vocabulary. When you own a business and are hiding from your psycho ex, you tend to not take a day off.

He turns to me and places a gentle kiss on my forehead, cupping my face in his hands. "We've got you covered, Princess. Let us take care of you."

My insecurities flare, and I wrap my hands around his wrists, holding him in place. "Us?"

"Yes, us."

"*Is* there an us? You and me?"

So much for not defining the relationship.

He gives me a half smile. "For as long as you're here, there will be an us."

My brows pinch. "As long as I'm here? Do you think I'm going to leave?"

"I think it's your instinct, and instincts are hard to fight."

He's pushing again.

"I think you're afraid, and I think it's because of Rachel." His body tenses at my accusation, letting me know that I'm right. "You don't have to tell me who she is, but don't make me pay for her sins."

He closes the distance and lightly brushes his lips against mine, then rests our foreheads together. "Sometimes it feels like you see too much."

I chuckle. "I feel the same way about you three."

We jump apart when there's a pounding on the door. Asher grabs the kitchen knife while Rio and Zane jump from the couch, each with handguns at the ready, before moving to peek out the front window.

"We got a runner," Zane observes, then bolts out the front.

"Shit," Rio shouts as he jumps over something on his way out.

I dart around Asher and run to the open door. The sun has begun setting and is right in my eyes, causing me to squint down at the dark lump on the front steps.

"Spencer!" Asher shouts from behind me.

"Oh my God," I gasp and throw a hand over my mouth, holding down the bile threatening to make an appearance.

On the steps is a bruised and bloodied teenage girl. There are two bullet holes in her body.

One in the heart, one in the skull.

"No," I whisper.

Asher grabs my shoulders and turns me around. I bury my face in his chest and squeeze my eyes shut, but the image is branded in my brain.

The girl is young, maybe in her teens, and holding a bouquet of purple hyacinths with multiple knives sticking out of her stomach.

CHAPTER 27

RIO

onight is not going how I imagined it. We were supposed to have a calm evening with dinner and maybe a nice fuck fest to soothe Spencer after the shit show outside the FBI. But no. Now Zane and I are chasing some motherfucker down the street who dropped a dead body on our doorstep.

Way to ruin the mood, pendejo.

The idiot dashes down an alley. Zane follows, which means it's my job to cut him off. I double my effort, lengthening my stride.

Should've done more running with Spencer.

I turn the corner and come up to where the alley spits back out onto a main street. Thankfully, the perpetrator emerges in front of me. On my next step, I launch myself forward and tackle the guy to the ground. We roll a few times when the sound of a click echoes on the street. Zane stands over us with his gun pointed at the guy.

"Fuck! I think you broke my arm!"

"Don't be such a baby; I highly doubt it's broken. If we're

complaining, then you got Spencer's favorite pants dirty." I wrestle him under me and get his hands behind his back. I stand and pull him to his feet with me.

A streetlamp gives us little light, but the big "13" on the back of his neck in gothic script stands out like a damn neon sign.

"You've got to be fucking kidding me! MS-thirteen?"

Zane moves to stand next to me to get a better view. "Fucking Gabriel."

"I highly doubt he knows about this."

"He's probably behind the whole thing." Zane glares at the guy's neck.

"We both know he's not. Now let's get this trash back to the house."

Zane presses the end of the barrel to the guy's back. "Make a sound and I'll put one in the back of your skull. I don't care who hears it."

The guy responds by standing taller and puffing up his chest. He's a few inches shorter than us with not a lot of meat on his bones. He's nowhere near intimidating, and all this posturing is rather annoying.

We make it back to the house without incident and tie the man up in the basement. Spencer doesn't ask questions or anything when we get back with a man at gunpoint. She's huddled on the couch with a cup of tea in her hands and a blanket around her shoulders.

"I called it in," Asher says by way of greeting. He's standing century at the back of the sofa, ensuring no nefarious person can get to Spencer.

"Did you check the note?" I ask.

Spencer pops out of her stupor and stands. "What note?"

Asher gestures for Spencer to sit back down. "Spencer—"

"I want to see it," she interjects.

"Mama, I don't think that's such a good idea."

Spencer sets down her mug with vigor. "Why not? We all know who did this!"

Zane grabs Spencer's hand. "You shouldn't touch the evidence until we know for sure."

"Fuck this." Spencer shoves Zane into me, and we tumble backward into the bar stools.

"Princess," Asher cautions. Spencer ignores the warning and fakes right then left. Asher falls for her tactics and trips. Spencer runs around the couch and straight for the body.

"Shit!" Asher grunts.

"*Mierda*," I complain.

Zane is the first one to get to Spencer just as she's plucking the greeting card from the bouquet. She kicks her legs wildly as Zane lifts her off her feet from behind. She refuses to let go of the card as Asher and I attempt to get it out of her hands.

"You fucking cavemen!" she wails.

As frustrating as this display of rebellion is, it's a little too hot to ignore. Her determination. Her fire. It has me hard in my slacks.

When Asher reaches for the card again, Spencer snaps her teeth at him. "I'll spank your ass raw if you bite me, Princess."

"Try it, see what happens, big guy!"

I sigh. "Just let her read it."

"Fuck. Fine." Asher runs a hand through his hair.

Spencer rips open the envelope and reads silently to herself.

"Well?" Asher asks impatiently.

Spencer's face turns ashen as she scans the card over and over. "It's for all of us."

CHAPTER 28

SPENCER

Detective Kingston, I believe you've been looking for this. Cain didn't get nearly as much out of her as he could have, but we figured you deserved a little present after I messed with your things once.

Former prosecutor Flores, here are your knives back. Sorry they're not clean.

Special Agent Dawson, I didn't like what your notes said about me. It's not nice to call someone a narcissistic psychopath with maternal trauma.

My sweet Flower, you smell just as wonderful as I remember. But if you let them touch you again, your punishment will be worse than last time.

My heartbeat stumbles over its own rhythm, and my palms turn sweaty. When did he smell me?

You already know.

After Rio and I . . . ? No, it's not possible. We've all been here. How could he have gotten into the house?

My men surround me and read over my shoulder.

"Fuck!" Asher shouts and paces the entryway.

"*Hijo de puta!*" *Son of a bitch!*

Zane seethes silently on the side.

I turn to him first. "Do you know her?"

He glares at the letter like he can set it on fire with his mind. "Her name is Ava Thomas. I've been looking for her since last month. She went missing outside a bodega in Chelsea. I figured Cain took her, but I guess Cain gave Ava to Anthony to send us a message."

"How did he 'mess with your things'?"

"I couldn't find my badge the other day. When I got to work, it was sitting in my desk drawer. I figured I left it there, but this letter means Anthony was in our house and took it."

"And when he says Cain didn't get much out of her . . ."

"Cain is a human trafficker we've been hunting for the last few years. He came out of nowhere and rose quickly. We know he and Anthony are friends. And what he means is selling her. She was probably a virgin, so he sold her virginity to the highest bidder."

My stomach turns, and rage coats my skin. This is what he does? This is why they kill people? I think I truly get it now. My own hands vibrate with the need to wrap them around Cain's throat and squeeze the life out of him. To sell another human being for profit and to take something that isn't his to take and give away . . . It's absolutely despicable.

How can someone be so entitled that they think they can

own another person the way someone owns a pair of jeans? As if they can use them and lend them out at their leisure. As individuals, we have autonomy! And Anthony thinks it's okay to swoop in and steal that from someone?

Fuck that and fuck him.

Rio finally speaks up and punches a hole in the wall by the stairs. "I think he was here more than once. Those are my knives in her stomach."

We all turn to Asher, searching for his explanation of the letter. He stops his pacing for a minute to give us an answer. "I found a few of my notes on the floor when I came downstairs a few nights ago. I guess that was him."

Lastly, they turn to me as Asher inquires, "What did he mean by 'you smell just as wonderful'?"

My mouth goes dry as a desert, and I attempt to moisten my brittle lips. "When I came downstairs, and y'all were listening to the recording . . . I had woken up without my pants on."

All my men go unnaturally still.

"Ex-fucking-cuse me?" Asher's growl makes me freeze.

Zane refuses to look me in the eye. "Did . . . Did he . . . Were you . . ."

"No. I don't think so."

"We're leaving," Asher proclaims and grabs me by the arm to march upstairs. Rio and Zane follow us without argument.

I, however, am not so amiable. I don't fight him as he pulls me along, but my words are sharp. "And where the hell are we supposed to go?"

"Your place." He says it like I was already supposed to know.

"But he knows where that is. Anthony could get to us there too." I give my statement with a "no duh" sort of delivery. I may not be the smartest in the room, but I'm no idiot and don't need to be talked to like I am. I know Anthony better than all three of them combined. "When Anthony is determined, there's no stopping him. He once secretly bought up shares in a man's business over the course of a year. Once he had a majority, he had the board vote him out and then drove the company into the ground all because the man had bested him in a game of poker."

Asher opens Zane's door and leads me inside while remaining in the hallway. "We can be just as determined, Spencer. Trust me. Now get packing. We'll leave as soon as the crime scene techs get here." He shuts the door in my face, and I hear his footsteps head back downstairs.

I guess I'm not winning this argument.

Spencer, one. Asher, one.

CHAPTER 29

ZANE

hen the FBI crime scene techs arrive, I go up to my room to pack my own bag. While we waited, we could all hear Spencer upstairs loudly yammering on to herself about "stupid entitled men."

I can only hope she wasn't referencing us.

Entering the room, I find her clothes strewn about and hanging off various décor like my bedside lamp and the 1999 signed and framed Knicks poster on the wall. Almost every piece of clothing we have for her here are off the hangers. Spencer stands with her back to me, just inside the closet door.

"Everything okay in here?"

She turns to me, finally showing me the item in her hands. She looks down at it as if I'm supposed to exclaim, "Oh no! How did that get there?" I give her a deadpan look instead.

"Well?!" she yells.

"Well, what?" I reply.

"What the hell is this?"

I scrunch my brows together. "It's your sculpture."

She rolls her eyes and stomps her foot. "I know that! I mean, what the hell is it doing here?"

"I bought it," I state matter-of-factly.

"Why!"

"Let me make this clear, Angel." I prowl towards her as she backs into the wall. "No one else gets that piece of you. No one else gets to see this side. Anyone who already has is lucky I'm letting them live with the memory, because if I thought you'd forgive me, I'd end every last person who's been in the gallery. Anyone who may have had a glimpse at your soul."

Spencer's breathing increases, and her cheeks flush. "Oh."

I lean down and bring our faces close together. "You're mine, Spencer Gray. In this life and the next."

Her rapid breaths cause her round tits to brush against my chest. "Why do you call me 'Angel'?"

My answer is easy. "You're the light I've never been afforded in life."

"Dammit. How do you always have the right thing to say?" Spencer moves fast, grabbing my face and bringing her mouth to mine.

I'm stunned for a split second before I react. My arms wrap around her waist, sealing our connection.

Spencer breathes out, "I need you. Now. Right now." Her hands go right to my pants and undo my belt. Her enthusiasm makes my dick grow hard.

She pulls my pants down to my hips then rips down her own pants. I let her keep the lead for one more moment. When she tries to climb me like a tree, I spin her so she faces the wall.

"You want me to fuck you, Angel? I'll fuck you like the glorious Angel you are." My hands wander to her breasts, each a perfect handful, and I give them a squeeze. "I'll worship these." One hand skims down her torso and covers her pussy.

"And I'll worship this, every day, for the rest of forever. This pussy, this ass, these tits, they're mine."

Her arousal floods my hand, and she whimpers. "Fuck yes."

I bend at the knees and line my cock up with her weeping core. When I thrust inside, she cries out, but I cut off the sound by wrapping my hand around her mouth.

"Don't be a bad Angel by letting the people downstairs hear your precious screams. Those are mine too."

Her moan fills the room, making my cock leak. Her dripping pussy allows my dick to glide in and out of her core so easily. Her hands claw at the wall, grasping for purchase. I begin a rhythm that has us groaning in unison, and she matches me thrust for thrust. Her sweet ass slams backward, making my cock unbearably hard each time it jiggles.

"Fuck, Baby. You look so divine just like this—impaled on my thick cock and whining for more."

Her pussy chokes my length each time I bury myself inside her.

"You're going to come with me, Spencer. Come with me and make that cunt suck me dry."

When her hand snakes between her legs, she rubs her clit. She screams behind my hand as her inner muscles contract around my cock as she comes. Her orgasm pulls me right under the wave of pleasure with her. I pound away, drawing out our high.

When the last drop of cum is wrung out of my dick, I fall forward on my hands so as not to crush Spencer against the wall.

"Holy shit," she exhales and smiles at me from over her shoulder.

I smirk right back at her. "Yeah, Angel. Holy shit."

CHAPTER 30

RIO

Zane and Spencer think they're being quiet, but they're fucking not. Literally fucking, and not quiet at all. I've been drowning out their moans by talking at an unusually louder volume about the most random shit so that no one can hear them.

I expect compensation in the form of foot massages and possibly blow jobs. Spencer would be mortified if she knew that we could hear her, and Zane would kill any living thing that heard her, so I'm doing them both a solid.

When their moans and cries finally end, I take out my phone and dial a number I wish I didn't have to. I mean, really. The fucker is apparently involved or wants to be involved with my little sister. Not to mention his two sidekicks.

Gabriel answers the phone a little too cheery. "*¿Que pasa, hermano?*"

"We need to talk," I retort.

"If this is about Carmen, it's not open to discussion."

I pace the kitchen. "Whatever you *think* you have going on with my sister, ends now. You leave her alone. She's not someone you can just fuck and ditch. I will cut you to pieces and scatter them across the Atlantic for the sharks if you so much as make her shed a single tear."

"Ooo. Brother Bear is in full swing." His sarcasm isn't amusing.

"I'm serious, Gabe. Leave her alone. She's way too young for you and doesn't need you dragging her down. She's in school. She's going places."

"Isn't your little side piece the same age as Carmen? And you and I are the same age, so . . ." He trails off, clarifying his innuendo.

"Spencer is none of your business," I spit out through gritted teeth.

"Uh huh. Sure. Well, this has been lovely, but I gotta—"

"This isn't why I called," I interrupt him.

His exasperated tone comes through the speaker. "Get to the point."

"You have a problem in your house."

"What are you talking about?"

"Cain is using more of your guys to do his bidding. I have one of your homeboys in my basement. He dropped a body on my porch as a warning from Cain and his friend."

"*Pendejo*," he mutters angrily.

"Yeah. You need to get your shit in order. It sounds like some of your guys aren't happy with how you're running things if they're looking outside *la mara* for work."

"Consider it taken care of. I'll send Diego and Mateo by to pick him up."

"We're doing a temporary move into the city. I'll leave a key under the doormat."

"I'll be sure to water your plants," Gabriel replies sarcastically then hangs up.

Asher approaches me in the kitchen with his partners,

Berkowitz and Kowalski. I've never learned their first names and never intend to. Asher never calls them by their first names, anyway.

Their expressions are serious, as always, but there's a different feel to the energy in the air this time.

Before I can ask what's going on, Asher gets right to the point. "The DNA results are back."

"From the Butcher and Spencer's attacker?"

He nods. "They're the same."

"Fuck me." I tip my head back and stare at the ceiling as if it's supposed to have all the answers written out plainly for me right there. "What should we do next?"

"The plan hasn't changed. We were operating under the assumption that Anthony and the Bride Butcher were the same person, and now we know for sure that's true."

Berkowitz gives his two cents. "If anything, now we'll all be more prepared."

"We?" I raise my brows at Asher.

"Yes, *we*. Berkowitz and Kowalski are going to help keep an eye on Spencer when needed."

"Okay . . . ?"

Asher turns to his partners. "Can you two find out how much longer the crime scene techs will be?"

They look at each other, confused, and then Kowalski speaks up. "Sure thing, man."

Once they're out of earshot, I whisper, "What the hell? You said the leak was one of them. Why are you letting them get closer?"

"So I can figure out which one it is," he says like that's the obvious answer.

"Spencer could get hurt in the process," I hiss.

He places a hand on my shoulder to soothe my worries.

"We'll take extra precautions. Between the three of us, we'll keep her safe."

"That better be how it goes down. She's been through enough. She doesn't need more shit piled on her."

Asher's face turns hard and determined. "Spencer is ours, and we protect what's ours."

CHAPTER 31

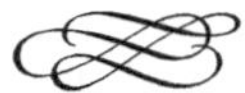

SPENCER

Packing my things was quick. Rio and Zane insisted I bring all the clothes they bought me, but fortunately, I was only able to fit so much in my bag. I carried Abuela's urn in my lap on the drive through downtown and to my apartment, which was uneventful, thank God.

After the last couple of days, I need some normalcy. I suppose it's a new normal I'm seeking, seeing as how I've agreed to stay.

We brought both Asher's Camaro and Zane's Honda. How they'll both find parking, I'm not sure, but I'm telling myself that's their problem. Not mine.

When we arrive the next morning, Asher and Rio go upstairs to my apartment to clear each room, leaving Zane and I standing on the sidewalk with my duffle.

"Do we have to stay here, or can we go inside Abstract Dreams while we wait?"

Zane frowns and nods his head. "Yeah, we can go inside."

"Awesome!" Grabbing my duffle, I heft it up over my shoulder.

"I can get that if you want," Zane suggests as he slings his own bag over his shoulder.

"No, I got it."

I know Zane is just being chivalrous, but my bag isn't that heavy, and I'm not a dainty person. *I am woman, hear me roar* and all that.

Zane does the gentlemanly thing and holds the door open for me, but when I step over the threshold, my bag gets caught on the doorjamb. Instead of stopping and assessing the situation like a normal person, I yank on my strap. When the bag doesn't come free, I yank one more time and fall through the doorway.

Righting myself, I realize my bag feels a bit lighter. I look down and find that my clothes litter the entryway of Abstract Dreams, and right on top are my colorful lacy intimates.

"Oh my God!" I dive for the pile on the floor.

Zane kneels down next to me and starts gathering my clothing. "It's not a big deal, Spencer. Nothing I haven't seen before," he says with a wink.

A fucking wink.

"So?! Anyone could walk in and see! Oh my God! I'm a business owner. If a customer walked in right now, they'd see my damn underwear all over the floor. I would have to kiss professionalism goodbye, and my name in the art community would be ruined! I'd have to start creating under a false name and take on a weird quirk like eating my hair. And trust me, you won't want me anymore when I become a hair eater."

Zane loses himself to a full-blown laughing fit.

I shove his shoulder, and he falls on his side to the floor. "Zane! This isn't funny!"

Through his laughter he's able to get out, "Yes, it is."

"My distress shouldn't be funny to you." I pout.

"I'm sorry, Angel. But eating hair? You expect me not to

laugh at that." He takes a deep breath and sighs with a huge smile as he grabs my face gently and gives me a quick kiss. "You're adorable. Now, let's shove the clothes in your bag. We can stash it behind the desk until we go upstairs."

Of course, he easily finds a solution.

What life must be like when you have a clear head . . .

A frazzled Iris steps out of the break room. Her hair is a mess, and her clothes are more casual than normal. She chews on the end of a pen as her gaze flicks back and forth between her phone and the floor.

"Oh my God! Spencer!" Iris jolts and dashes over to me. "Where have you been? I've been so worried about you!" She pulls me up as her arms wrap around me. Her hug feels weaker than normal.

I place my hands on her shoulders and lean back. "What do you mean? I thought . . ."

She winces at my touch, pulling out of our embrace. Her eyes almost bug out of her head when she sees Zane standing behind me, but she recovers quickly. "Yeah, yeah. You were busy finally getting your donut hole glazed."

I ignore her joke and get right to the point. "Iris, are you okay?"

"I'm fine." She smiles wide, but when we're this close, I can see the bags under her eyes and the lack of makeup on her skin.

"You don't seem fine." I reach for her hand, but she flinches away. "Iris, what's going on?"

She waves her hand in the air. "Nothing. He's, I mean, I've been worried about you."

"Hayes?"

"Yeah, Hayes. He's been doing fine running the studio, but we've been worried, is all."

"I thought—"

Iris moves back to the front desk and snags her purse, slinging it over her shoulder. "Well, I should get going. So happy you're back! Bye!" She darts out the door before Zane, or I can say goodbye back.

"Is she okay?" Zane asks next to me.

"I don't know. Maybe my leaving for a week was too much. I should have checked in with her."

Zane tilts his head. "We took your phone, Spencer. How would you have called her?"

"I don't know. I just feel responsible." My shoulders slump forward.

He slings his arm around me. "She'll be okay. Now let's go say hi to Hayes and everyone else."

Opening the door to Clay Creations is much easier than normal. When I make a confused face, Zane just shrugs and ushers me through the door.

"Spencer!" Hayes rushes to me and picks me up in an all-encompassing hug. My heart contracts and if I were the Grinch, I'm sure this is the point where it would grow three times its size. I hug him back just as hard and tears line my eyes. I knew that if I left, I'd miss this, but getting to hug them all again really makes the thought hit home.

When Hayes sets me down, Alma and Paul take their turns hugging me. "It's only been a week, y'all." I know my comments make me sound put out, but I'm over the moon that I get to see them all again.

"How was your self-discovery?" Alma asks, then raises her brows up and down. "Did any of *them* help with your little introversion excursion?"

My cheeks are set aflame as I flounder for a response. Alma beats me to the punch though. "Ahh. Good for you, *chica*," she says with a wink.

"Leave her alone, Alma." Paul leads Alma back to their wheels.

"Boss, you'll be happy to know I've had everything under control. Inventory has been counted, more dates with the kids' summer camp have been set, the storage closet is organized, kiln time has been scheduled, and I've begun a list of things we may need to order soon."

My cheeks become wet from tears falling down my face.

Hayes's face turns alarmed, and he looks to Zane for help. "Uh. Spencer? Are you okay? Have you been watching videos of lost pets reuniting with their owners again? You know what happened last time you did that."

"No, no. Sorry. I'm fine." I wave him and Zane off.

Hayes looks unconvinced but doesn't push the topic further. "Okay. But did you get the inspiration you needed?"

My mind goes over everything I learned and went through in the last week. I learned some truths that have been hard to accept, but they were truths I needed to absorb and understand. While I'll never understand Anthony, I see him in a clearer light.

I smile at Hayes as ideas begin popping into my mind. "You know what? I think I did."

CHAPTER 32

SPENCER

The rest of the day, and over the next several days, I work tirelessly on my pieces for the exhibit. Zane and Rio fall right back into the routine we had set before. They both go to work and then meet me for lunch. Asher glues himself to my side, but this time it's way more pleasant.

Kind of.

Whenever I need a break at the Mudhouse, Asher tags along. The giant and I practically become Siamese twins! But he's still holding back. At night, Zane and Rio squeeze themselves in my bed with me. Asher insists it'd be weird for him to sleep in the room with us. I offered solutions, but he's slept on my couch every night instead.

All three of them have tried sneaking peeks at my sculptures, but I shoo them away every time by flinging wet clay at them and then cover the piece with a towel. I know they'll see them when they're on display soon, but if they don't like my art, I don't want to know. I'm not going to be able to watch them watch the reveal. I think I'll hang out in the corner with a paper bag instead.

Eight days of being covered in clay is exactly what I needed to feel normal again—I feel right at home. The ideas in my brain flow right from my mind through my fingertips and into the clay. Each design is an expression of my soul. Vulnerability and doubt constantly make appearances in my consciousness, but I battle them away by trudging through.

It's Thursday night, and I'm standing in the middle of ten completed sculptures. Alma and Paul left this afternoon, and I sent Hayes home a few hours ago. The three of them are the only ones I've allowed to see my sculptures. They've all given me usable criticism that I think has made this exhibit my best one yet.

My relief is tangible.

I take another moment to revel amidst my accomplishments. "I finished."

Asher looks up from his laptop and eyes all of the covered pieces of art. He leans back in his too-small-for-him stool against the worktable and loosely crosses his arms. "Umm. Are the towels part of the exhibit?"

A chuckle involuntarily escapes me. "No."

Asher smiles and shrugs his shoulders. "Then show them to me."

I fake giving his demand actual thought. "Mmm. No thanks. You can see them for the first time tomorrow like everyone else."

Asher's glare holds little heat. "You're being a brat."

"And I'm not ashamed."

He sets his laptop aside and stands to his full height. He swaggers up to me, his body almost touching mine but not quite. His heat seeps into my bones, but I hold myself back.

"Hey guys! I forgot my sketchbook." Hayes's interruption triggers Asher to spring back from me. Hayes ignores the fact that he found us in a slightly precarious position and snags his sketchbook. He exits, leaving Asher and me in an awkward silence.

He's still holding back, and I don't know why. I have my suspicions, but I have a feeling that with a man like Asher, I won't be able to dig the truth out of him.

Asher rubs the back of his neck. "You ready for tomorrow?"

"Um, as ready as I'll ever be, I guess. Iris has been hard at work getting the word out about the exhibit. And I think opening it up to Paul, Alma, and Hayes has helped generate more interest."

"Cool. We should go upstairs. You'll need your rest for tomorrow." Asher shuts the studio down for me then guides me out the door. He doesn't let me clean up or anything.

The hurt on my face is impossible to hide, but Asher doesn't give any indication that he notices.

He said he's in it for as long as I'm here, and I plan on being here for the long haul.

But he doesn't believe me . . .

It's ten minutes until the doors open, and just like I predicted, I'm standing in the corner. The only thing I don't have is the paper bag, which I asked Rio to get me, but he told me he has a better option than a paper bag. His eyes turned lustful, and I had to walk away.

Sleep last night was unattainable. Now lightheadedness and dizziness are two consorts that I can't shake. If I bite at my lips anymore, I'm sure they'll bleed.

"Breathe, Angel. It's going to be fine. Everything looks

amazing." Zane strokes my hair as his other hand wanders down to my ass.

"Not helping," I snap as I jump out of his reach, even though heat begins to build low in my belly.

"I can't help it when you look this delicious." His eyes wander up and down my frame.

Each of my men dressed up tonight. Asher is wearing what looks to be a work suit. Zane is in black slacks and a white button-up. Rio is in all black with the top few buttons of his shirt undone, giving me an enticing peek at his tattoos. Both Zane and Rio rolled up their sleeves.

I never thought I'd be an arm girl, but here we are.

Maybe you're more of an Asher, Rio, and Zane girl.

When I was shopping online for tonight, I chose a simple dress that I hope screams sexy but not in a distracting way. It's a strapless, knee-length, satin, black dress with an A-line skirt and sweetheart neckline. I found deep green heels and curled my hair into waves to complete the look.

Okay, Alma curled my hair. Iris was unable to help with my makeup, so I was left to my own devices and had a little help from YouTube.

Iris is now running around the gallery, spouting off instructions to the waitstaff and making sure everything is in its place. She seems a bit more stressed than normal, possibly because this is the first exhibit she's in charge of. But she's done a wonderful job. I keep reassuring her of her amazing work, but each time she walks away more distraught than before. Even Hayes's attempts and comfort have been for naught.

Alma and Paul are cool as fucking cucumbers. Alma said her kids are coming with her husband, and Paul said his neighbors were excited to see his work.

"T-minus two minutes!" Iris calls out, then scurries off to the breakroom where the caterers have set up shop.

Zane grabs me by the shoulders and turns me to face him. "Spencer, you got this. You're talented and badass. Everyone is going to love your work." His eyes bore into mine, making me soak up the truth in his words.

Deep breaths bring my heart rate back to a normal pace. "Thank you," I say with a smile.

He kisses my forehead and adds, "I'm so proud of you, Angel."

His assertion hits me straight in the chest, causing spontaneous tears to form in my eyes. I hold them back because I did not spend an hour on this makeup to fuck it up now. That and I don't think I can answer the "have you been crying" question all night long with the "it's just allergies" practiced response.

The doors open, and I pat lightly under my eyes. Rio makes his way to my side and grasps my hand in his. His excitement is indisputable. Asher stands by the door, subtly inspecting every patron who walks through the door.

I recognize Alma's family, a few of the baristas from the Mudhouse, and some of the customers who come by Abstract Dreams regularly. But there are even more people I don't recognize—people who look at each sculpture, vase, teapot, and jar with wonder and fascination.

Then, in walks Joey, and the waterworks pick up all over again. He's wearing a tweed brown suit with a white shirt and deep maroon tie. We make eye contact, and I move to him as fast as one can in heels. I wrap my arms around him, shocking him. He takes a moment to adjust but then returns my embrace.

"Did you get where you needed to go, kid?"

I lean back, our arms still around each other. I glance over my shoulder to Rio and Zane then Asher by the door. "Yeah, Joey. I did."

He gives me an endearing smile and then goes right back to business. "Good, because you look like shit."

"And you look like a shriveled-up dick," I reply through my tears.

"Now, let's talk about you skipping out on your workouts."

Laughing aloud, my nerves ease and I feel like I can finally breathe.

The next hour is spent mingling as consumers ask me every question under the sun.

Where did I get the idea for the sculpture of a bouquet of hyacinths and knives? What technique did I use for the high relief of women in shackles at an auction? Did Greek Cycladic figurines inspire the form of a dead woman with a hole in the chest and forehead?

I'm not sure how I answered each question. Those sixty minutes were a blur. My social meter is full and ready to burst. Asher is busy wandering the room, and not wanting to bother him, I sneak off to Clay Creations next door for a small reprieve.

When I shut the connecting door behind me, silence fills my ears, and I sag against it. Cleansing breaths fill my lungs as I breathe in the scent of dirt and clay, a smell that has always brought me peace, especially in the last few years.

The studio was closed all day today in preparation for the art show opening, so the floor is clean, the lights are dim, and all the stools are up on tables and pottery wheels. I take a stool off one of the canvas worktables and sink down onto it.

The door bursts open, and I almost fall out of the chair.

Asher shuts the door behind him and stomps over to me. "Goddammit, Spencer! You can't just walk off like that right now." He grabs my arm and pulls me out of the chair.

"Calm down, big guy. I just needed a moment to breathe.

There are a lot of people over there and, in case you haven't noticed, I don't do well in crowds for long periods of time."

He points to himself. "Then you get me. You get me, and I will take you somewhere. I thought you . . ." He cuts himself off.

My heart sinks. "You thought I had left."

He turns his head to the side. "Maybe."

Reaching up, I cup his cheeks in my hands and turn his face back to me. "I'm sorry. I didn't mean to scare you."

"I'm fine."

"I promise I will get you next time. I promise. Don't push me away."

He shakes his head. "I'm not."

My heels give me a few inches, but I'm still not as tall as Asher. I pull his face to mine and give him a brief kiss. "Yes, you are. Please don't be afraid of me."

"I'm not," he repeats himself, emphasizing his earlier argument.

I give him a sad smile. "Repeating the words doesn't make it true."

His eyes meet mine. "I'm trying, Princess."

"That's all I can ask for."

We both lean into each other and our lips meet in a kiss where we finally aren't battling for control. It's a kiss of comfort, a kiss of reassurance. Reassurance that I'm here.

Laughter fills the room, and Asher and I break our kiss. His brows are scrunched while the hair on the back of my neck stands on end.

I know that laugh. I know it too well.

My head turns to the back of the studio, and Anthony makes his presence known by walking into the light.

But he's not alone. He's accompanied by five men, all with

guns raised and pointed at Asher and me. My mouth falls open, and a chill sweeps over me. My hands shake uncontrollably.

Anthony's smile is wide. Too wide. "Special Agent Asher Dawson, it's a pleasure to finally meet you. Now, please take a step away from my fiancée and keep your hands where I can see them."

Asher raises his hands in front of his person but steps in front of me, hiding me from Anthony and obeying only half of the demand. The lock on the door connecting Clay Creations and Abstract Dreams locks into place.

"You should know better than to come between a man and his love." Anthony's voice holds a warning in it. A warning I know he won't give twice.

"If you had any claim over her, I might step aside. But I know how much she hates you. I know how much you disgust her. She'll never want you."

"You don't know what you're talking about. My Flower loves me. That bitch fucking worships me! This has all been a test. She just wanted to know how much I love her, and I've proven it many times over again."

Oh my God. He really is insane. I'm not going to walk away this time. He's going to drag me back, kicking and screaming, and he'll pay everyone to look the other way.

Another gun clicks. "Last time, Dawson. Step aside."

I grab Asher's arm and grip it hard. "Asher, just—"

A loud bang echoes through the room and causes a ringing in my ears. Asher grunts and falls to his knees. My body freezes as I watch the shoulder on Asher's shirt turn red with blood. I open my mouth to shout, but no sound comes out.

Muffled screams come from the other side of the door.

Anthony moves to stand in front of Asher and points his gun right at Asher's forehead. Asher stares down the barrel without fear. The vein in his temple twitches as he looks on at Anthony in pure hatred.

"NO!" I finally cry out and jump in front of Asher.

Anthony's reaction is immediate. He raises his hand and slaps me hard across the face. I fall to the side.

"Don't you ever come between me and my kill ever again!" Anthony turns to his men. "Grab her. The other two are going to be in here any second." He looks at Asher one more time. "Him too. He's coming along to answer some questions." Anthony leans down so he's at eye level with Asher and smiles. "This is going to be so much fun."

Foreign arms wrap around my torso and lift me off the ground. I kick and scream but to no avail.

Someone pounds on the connecting metal door. "Spencer! Spencer!" Zane's shouts make their way through the door, but his person doesn't follow. That door is thick and sturdy. They're not getting through but are making their best effort.

Asher is hefted up by two men, one on each arm, and dragged through the back door and into a waiting white van with no windows. When I'm finally hauled through the back door, the front of the studio opens and Rio and Zane yell for me. We make eye contact as the door shuts. Tears drip from my chin, and terror enters their gazes as the sliding van door shuts and a black cloth bag is thrown over my head.

CHAPTER 33

SPENCER

The sound of fists meeting flesh and Asher's grunts of pain are stuck in my brain. As long as I live, I'll never get that sound out of my memory.

After a lifetime of driving, the van stops, and Asher and I are lugged into a building. As my body is dropped into a chair, the wood groans. The same sound echoes from my right as I assume Asher is set in an identical chair. My wrists and ankles are released but then quickly taped to the arms and legs of the chair.

The bag is removed from my head, and a bright, hanging light directly overhead blinds me momentarily as my eyes adjust.

A figure comes into my vision, blocking the light. "Flower, my Flower. I finally have you back right where you belong." Anthony's finger trails down the side of my face and across the top of my breasts.

I jerk my head to the side to get away from his touch. Asher's beaten body sags in the chair next to me, and my stomach drops. The hors d'oeuvres I consumed earlier are ready to come back up, but I force the food to stay in my stomach.

The rest of the room comes into view. It's spacious and sparsely lit with some wooden crates in the corner. Earthy scents fill my nose. The ceiling is high, at least twenty feet or higher. The windows are only along the wall's top three feet or so. The walls are red brick, and the floor is made of smooth, dark gray concrete. I think it's safe to assume we're in a warehouse somewhere in New York or New Jersey, based on how long it took us to get here. The air isn't as humid as Manhattan, but humid enough that I feel like I'm wearing a hot wet blanket.

Asher's left eye is swollen shut and blood trickles from his nose. Sweat drips from his hairline as his body slumps forward. His clothes are in disarray and soaked in blood and sweat.

"What did you do to him?" I ask while whimpering.

Anthony grips my chin too hard and turns my face back to him. "Ignore him. He doesn't matter anymore now that I'm here."

He dared to touch what's mine.

Asher is mine.

My knuckles turn white as I clutch the arms of the chair, and my voice lowers. "What the fuck did you do to him?"

Anthony's hand flies across my face again, and he leans down to whisper threateningly in my ear. "You'll do well to remember not to speak to me that way."

"Leave her alone," Asher gets out between panting breaths.

Hearing his struggle renews my vigor. Whipping my head to the side, I butt my forehead into his nose. Anthony's hand flies to his face, and blood streams down his mouth. "I will speak to you however I want! You don't touch him ever again! Let us go!"

Anthony uses the handkerchief from his pocket to help

staunch the bleeding. "You're going to learn your place again, Flower. Don't worry. I know just how to do that."

His hands go for his belt buckle. The clink of metal causes nausea to whirl in my stomach. He whips off the leather with a crack and undoes his pants.

"Remember what I taught you before? You're going to give me exactly what I want. Now don't move."

My mind and body freeze as he wraps the belt around my throat, yanking my head into a bow. He lowers his pants just enough to allow his erect dick to slip free.

"Open."

Before he can force me to comply, a young man rushes through the door, barely out of adolescence. "Boss! Boss!" When he reaches us, Anthony spins with a punch to the kid's gut.

Through gritted teeth, Anthony hisses, "Never interrupt me when I'm training, Jackson. You should have been informed of that."

Jackson rolls onto his hands and knees and wheezes. "Sorry, Boss. Mr. Murphy sent me in. He said he's urgent."

Anthony turns to one of his men, giving instructions to stay with us and the rest are to set a perimeter around the building.

When everyone leaves except our guard, I whisper discreetly to Asher, waking him. "Are you okay?"

"Right as rain, Princess." His words are tired, and I know he's trying to make the situation seem less severe.

"We're going to be okay. I'll find us a way out of here."

"The guys will come for us. We just have to hold on until they get here. It won't be long."

Dear God, I can only hope he's right.

CHAPTER 34

SPENCER

*A*sher falls asleep reluctantly. His slouched position can't be comfortable, but I highly doubt he'll complain. I had to reassure him over and over that I would be fine and that he needed the rest. His skin is ghostly white from the blood loss from his gunshot wound.

I should sleep too, but I can't relax my body enough to slide into unconsciousness. My face hurts from the two hits, so I can't imagine how much pain Asher must be in.

Before falling asleep, Asher said I need to play along with whatever Anthony says and does. He said I need to play into Anthony's fantasy—that I appreciate the dead women and that I've been testing him to see how much he really cared. He said anything within reason will help keep us alive longer. Asher wouldn't sleep until I promised I'd try.

I'm not sure how I'm going to pull it off. Zane, Rio, and Asher said I wear my heart on my sleeve, but to ensure our survival, I will do my best.

Watching as the moon recedes from the sky and the sun rises over the horizon, I log everything I notice and commit every detail to memory. The guards rotate posts in the room three times; each new guard is a man I don't recognize as one of the five who showed up at Clay Creations. I hear multiple footsteps and light conversation outside the window twenty-four times. Not once do I hear car horns, trains, boats, or water.

The door creaks open when the sunlight shines directly through the windows. Not very high in the sky so it's not noon yet.

"Asher," I shout-whisper in an attempt to wake him. We're about three feet apart, so I'm praying a whisper is enough. "Asher."

In steps Anthony, Pierce, and more armed men. One of them drags a limp form by the shoulder. Both Anthony and Pierce wear expensive suits like they always do.

Anthony does a quick assessment of my being, but Pierce's eyes linger in the all the places I don't want them to. I know I look like a mess. I'm sweaty, and I'm sure my makeup is smeared all over my face.

One man carries a bucket and walks right up to Asher, dousing him in ice cold water. Some of the droplets land on my bare arm and cause goosebumps to instantly break out across my skin. Asher wakes with a blink then leans back into the chair.

Anthony speaks first. "Good morning. I hope your stay here last night was pleasant."

Asher's spark is back as he sizes up each man in the room. "I hope you're not planning on going into the hotel business because you will not get a great Yelp review from us."

Anthony smiles. "That's too bad. I recently purchased a small chain of hotels in Los Angeles." His attention turns to me while Pierce's focus hasn't strayed. "How did you sleep, My Flower?"

"Good. Thank you." I try to swallow, but my mouth is dry.

Anthony approaches me and squats down, so we're face to face. He raises his hand to touch my cheek, and I flinch back. "Don't be afraid of me. I've missed you so much, Flower." He snaps his fingers and another man with a bucket sets it down next to Anthony and hands him a small towel. "Let's clean you up a little bit. We have guests coming and a good fiancée should look presentable."

I clench my jaw and hold back my retort about how a good fiancé doesn't hurt their partner. Instead, I nod.

He hands his jacket to one of his men and rolls up his sleeves. On his forearm is a tattoo I know he didn't have three years ago. I subtly spot Asher out of the corner of my eye staring in shock at Anthony.

Anthony finally notices the object of my attention but doesn't stop cleaning my face with the wet towel. "Like it? I got it for you."

"For me?"

"Yes, Spencer. I always wanted the skull and snake, but I added the lilies for you. Spencer Lily Gray." Anthony pauses and looks to me expectantly.

"Thank you. I love it." My voice is hollow, but Anthony reacts like I just told him he's the love of my life.

"I knew you would." Satisfied with his work, he stands and puts his suit coat back on.

Asher clears his throat. "You're Cain." It's not a question.

Cain. The human trafficker that Rio, Zane, and Asher have been trying to capture. Anthony is Cain?

Anthony smiles a self-satisfied smile. "Actually, Pierce and I are both Cain. I'm disappointed you and your little annoying friends couldn't figure it out on your own."

Asher shakes his head. "You're a sick son of a bitch."

Anthony strikes fast, punching Asher in the face. Asher's

head whips to the side, but he doesn't give up. He laughs through the pain. "My, my. Someone is a little sensitive."

The door swings open, banging against the brick wall. "Where the hell have you been?!"

The blood drains from my face. What is she doing here? "Mom?"

"Spencer," Asher cautions.

"Don't speak to her!" Anthony yells at Asher.

My focus is glued to her. "Mom! How did you find me?"

Instead of listening to me, she ignores my question and stomps right over to Anthony. Her hair is perfectly curled and pinned back, and her makeup is pristine. She looks clean and put together in a beige sheath dress and black pumps. "You've been dodging my calls. Even Pierce won't answer me!"

Why is she calling Anthony and Pierce? Why isn't she trying to get to me? I need her help. I never wanted her caught in the middle, but we all need to get out of here.

"Mom! Please help me! My friend is hurt. We have to go!" But no one pays attention to me. Not even a whisper of a glance.

Anthony's mouth crimps and his teeth grind. "Who let you in, Mariana?"

Mom's arms wave around wildly at her outrage. "That's not important. I want to know why you're ignoring me! I did everything you asked. I got you her number, I gave you information about where she might be. Hell! I delivered her to you on a silver platter, and you couldn't even keep her in line!"

Who is "she"?

Anthony doesn't answer her but looks to the man closest to him and snaps his fingers then points at Mom. "Time to go, Mariana." The man grips Mom's upper arm.

"What are you doing? Get your dirty hands off me! Anthony, tell him to let me go."

"Mom!" I plead again.

She finally turns to me. "Oh my God! Shut up! You insufferable idiot! I needed you to do one thing. One damn thing! You couldn't give me this? You couldn't just marry him?"

"What are you talking about?"

Looking around the room, I notice how everyone is looking at me with varying expressions ranging from pity to glee.

My voice turns timid. "Mom? What's going on?"

"Spencer." Asher's voice is sympathetic.

"Don't 'Spencer' me! I need to keep my mom safe. I've worked hard to keep everyone safe," I snap at Asher.

Anthony speaks slowly as if speaking to a child. "The night we met, there was an auction."

I shake my head. "No, it wasn't an auction. It was an art show. My first art show."

Half of Anthony's mouth lifts. "No, Flower. It was an auction."

My mind is spinning. It was definitely an art show.

Am I going crazy?

"Where was the auction? Was it in a different room? What was being sold?"

Anthony's gaze turns possessive as he looks me right in the eye. "You."

"Me?" My hands tremble.

"I bought you and your sweet virgin blood. By right, you are mine. You were bought and paid for."

I was . . . sold?

"Mom?"

The click of her heels echo in the room as she walks right up to me. Her hands cover my wrists and tighten like a vice. "Why did you have to make this so hard? You've always been such a stupid fucking brat."

My heart shatters right there on the bitter concrete floor.

My muscles go weak. It's like an anesthetic is injected into every vein in my body as numbness takes over my limbs. But Mom doesn't wait for me to adjust.

"Your father didn't want anything to do with you, but at least he paid up. Then you were about to turn eighteen, and the nice cash flow was going to stop. I had to think of something. I met Anthony at a gala, and when he suggested an auction, I thought it was too good to be true. If I would have known he just wanted you for himself, I would've handed you right over. But he got one look at you, and he wanted you for more than one night. He wanted forever, so we came up with an arrangement."

My panting is the only sound in the room. Her face is the only thing in focus in my vision. Everything and everyone else is a blur.

The deafening sound of my brain splintering takes over my consciousness like nails on a chalkboard. The jagged pieces left behind can't be glued back together. The shards are barbed, tearing apart each happy childhood memory. Each nurturing moment.

She. Sold. Me.

"I gave Anthony every bit of information I could while you were off whoring yourself out to those lowlifes."

"My phone number?" My voice is empty.

"I had to. The only way Anthony would pay me was if I gave him anything useful."

"You *sold* me? Your child?"

She grits her teeth and spits more vile words my way. "You are nothing to me." She stands and runs her hands down her dress to straighten out the wrinkles. She addresses Anthony formally. "You have what you want. I expect my payments to resume as usual."

He nods with a smile, like she gave him water while he was

dying of dehydration. She willingly turns for the door and exits the room so easily, leaving me behind, in the hands of a madman.

The person who was hauled in earlier groans on the floor. The dark hair, painted nails, and pink heels scratch at a memory in my mind. But I'm unable to connect the dots until she rolls over.

Her face is covered in black and blue, her lip is cracked and bleeding, and her leg rests to her side at an odd angle.

"Iris?"

The Devils of New York story continues in *Veiled Vengeance*. Preorder your copy on Amazon by scanning the QR code below.

Want more of Rio, Asher and Zane? Get an exclusive bonus scene by scanning the QR code below.

ACKNOWLEDGMENTS

To my book husband—Book two is done. Your support is everything and what keeps me going. Your love, the late night coffee runs, calming cuddles, and words of praise are given freely. You always know what I need and have it ready before I even voice it. Thank you, thank you, thank you! I love you to the moon and back.

To my ride-or-die bitch—Here we are, all these years later. The Scorpio to my Cancer, the green witch to my moon witch. Your patience and loyalty are a cherished gift. Thank you for always being willing to lend me your listening ear and validating my every outlandish feeling, no matter how hormonal-induced they are. I look forward to the endless comedic reels. To the spirit of the bottlenose dolphin! I love you!

Savannah—Thank you for matching my crazy! The late nights watching true crime while we make bracelets, the endless support you give me, the unconditional love. I don't know if I have words that can express how grateful I am to have you in my life and how much I fucking love you.

Bestie Alexys—Thank you for letting me sit with you and pick your brain over every little detail. I swear our minds sync up and just link. Thank you for supporting me and getting excited with me! Love you!

Becca & Jill—Thank you for being my hype team! Every little doubt, every little negative remark, y'all have been there and battled them away with me. I wouldn't be able to do what I do without your support! Love you both like crazy! Moon & stars, baby!

Ashli & Beth—My night owl team! Your honesty and opinions push me. You two are the golden geese of alpha readers! I could not do this without you. Love you both!

Gal—Rio would not be who he is without you! Thank you for being my bookstagram friend, my bright light, and the encouraging and sympathetic voice when I needed to vent. Love you!

My siblings—Remember, this book does not exist. Mom and Dad will figure it out when we're all dead.

STAY CONNECTED

You can find Ivy in all the bookish places…
>Website
>Newsletter
>Ivy's Spicy Harem (Facebook Reader Group)
>Instagram
>Goodreads
>BookBub
>Amazon
>Pinterest
>Threads

ABOUT THE AUTHOR

Ivy King is a why choose dark romance author who lives in the mountains of Idaho with her book husband, four wild kids, and cuddly pitbull. When Ivy isn't writing smut, you can find her tending to her emotional support houseplants, wrapped in a fluffy blanket reading romance novels, doom scrolling on her phone, or watching true crime.